Simon Palomar

by

A. A. Villescas

Cover illustrated
by
Misael Armendariz

This story is true, as recalled by Simon Palomar. However names, some locations and some events have been altered for protection. Some occurrences have been changed for narrative ease.

*This book is dedicated
to all those who consider their childhood to have been
less than perfect.*

This story is true as recalled by Simon Palomar.

SIMON PALOMAR

Simon Palomar

1

(1964)

The man in the clean white jacket leaned over his desk, his head resting on his left hand and his right poised with a pen. His frown was easy to see above his steel glasses.

"You're just a kid—in seventh grade and I'm here to help you. What made you do it....?" He waited. Drops of sweat made his forehead gleam. He smiled with his lips forming a straight line.

Was it a trap? I looked behind him at the locked door. This man had the key.

Along one side of the room was a large mirror. When they brought me in I had passed through a hallway which had a glass window that looked into this room. From inside, I couldn't see out. I wondered who was watching behind the mirror.

"Simon, I can see you are very angry and together we can work on that." He tugged on his red-flowered tie. His hands were smooth and white, with no calluses.

I sat across from him on a small stool, my lips clenched together, quivering inside, still as a cornered rabbit, but determined to give nothing away. I knew his offer to help was not real.

On the desk was a triangular wedge of green plastic with the name, Dr. Gregory Z. Welch, printed in black.

"I want to get to know *you*, Simon. Tell me about yourself." He leaned forward.

I gave him a stony stare and remained motionless. When I didn't answer he jiggled a little in his seat and looked at the ceiling, then back at me.

Everyone has weaknesses. I could see this doctor did not like it at all when I did not talk or move. *Maybe I could use this as a wedge to sway the advantage a little my way.*

"Well, then, tell me about your family. What is your father like?" He pried.

That *was* a good question.

Many boys try to be like their father. I am not one of them. I never could figure him out. He was large and heavy and had huge, bear-like arms. He hardly ever talked. Through much of my life he seemed like a mute cardboard figure—bigger than life but seldom speaking to us.

Letters that came to the house he left unopened on the table. After I began to go to school I found out that he could not read and resented those of us who knew how. Every weekday he would stop up the street to spend time with his mother, Grandma Olivia, who thought he could do no wrong. He spent a lot of time in the evenings away with his friends. On weekends he was usually gone.

The noise level in the house dropped when he entered our house because he ruled with fear. He raised an eyebrow if someone was out of line. If he stared at us we knew there was going to be trouble. We learned never to cry when he took out his belt and attacked because if we did, he beat harder. He whipped all of his many children, boys and girls alike, except his favorite, his namesake eldest son, who was quiet, like him.

For some reason I could never understand, he seemed to hate me more than the others. I tried to please him and begged my mother to tell me the reason that I was especially hated. He would make me kneel and then lash me with his belt.

"Smile," he would demand.

Well, maybe that was one thing I had in life that I *could* thank him for—I could keep from crying and smile in almost any situation. *This doctor had little chance of cracking me.*

We lived on the fringes of El Paso, Texas. It is a special city—a border city in which many people speak Spanish, only; and many others speak two languages fluently.

Not far from our home the Rio Grande flowed. In the growing season it watered fields on both sides of the valley. If we crossed that river or walked to the west, we would be in the state of New Mexico. A little further down and across the river was the state of Chihuahua, Mexico. Before a fence was built it was easy to cross the border in town or in the desert. Smugglers of humans and goods flourished. Near Mount Cristo Rey the three states and two countries come together.

The Franklin Mountains divide the west and east sides of El Paso. We often saw deer and coyotes in the arroyos that brought rainwater gushing from the mountains in the rainy season.

Downtown El Paso held two bridges which led to Juarez, Mexico. Cars and pedestrians crossed back and forth all day and all night. In those years, in the daytime, throngs from both countries enjoyed shopping on the other side. The trolleys circled freely in a loop. For miles, the two cities bordered the Rio Grande, so close to each other one could easily toss a ball the distance. In some places, people found it possible to easily wade across. Many families had members on both sides.

A large number of the older ones in my neighborhood had crossed the border to escape the chaos of the Mexican Revolution. They helped each other. Some of the men found work in the fields or at the large smelter that was close to the river and to town. Most homes were small and built of adobe.

I was taught early in life to cry on the inside, only, and to fight. When my brothers and sisters roamed the neighborhood, together we formed a big troop, strong enough for others to be afraid of us. We were glad to go out along the dusty streets and see what our friends and neighbors were doing because there was not a lot to keep us home.

We had very few rules. We were just told that if we got into trouble—not to let it follow us home.

We lived in a tiny adobe hut with the three windows either broken or boarded up most of the time. My mother told me that she raised pigs to buy her own lot when she was in her teens. Later, when she married my father, she traded the lot for this one—that had walls and a roof. On one side she hung a large crucifix. On another wall she hung a mirror on a nail. When an electrical storm came we hurried to cover this and any other mirrors with a sheet to prevent them from attracting the lightning bolts.

There was no plumbing—inside or out. We brought water in pails from a neighbor's faucet next door, unless that family was mad at us—then, our water came from the Rio Grande. We had no lights, no electricity. Until I was ten the floor was entirely dirt. The younger ones could dig roads in it and play without going outside.

Occasionally, we dug a new hole for the outhouse and moved the wooden frame. Sears catalogues were popular as toilet paper.

The boys gathered wood and chopped it, early, for our mother to start the fire in the stove. She always rolled out a huge stack of tortillas in the morning. For this she used a large bowl and filled it from a twenty-five pound sack of flour. She added baking powder and salt, mixed in a little lard and then added water and kneaded it to make a dough. If there was time, she covered it with a cloth. Then she formed flattened balls in her hands and laid them out ready to roll. Sometimes she had a smooth dowel for rolling—other times she used a bottle.

She took pride in forming perfect circles and getting the griddle heated to just the right temperature. The girls helped flip and press them down as they bubbled up and cooked.

Every day she cooked a large pot of pinto beans. Then she used whatever she had at hand, adding chile, garlic, onions, or chorizo to them. My mother was the one who made it a home. She was almost always smiling and joking. She liked to tease.

Behind our house stretched miles of open desert between the river and the mountains. We ran about, barefoot, chasing jackrabbits, and lizards, watching out for cactus and rattlesnakes. We sat in the shade of scrubby mesquite trees, chewed on the bean pods, and sucked the honey from the flowers of the desert willow when it bloomed. A good summer rain would fill the air with the lemony scent of *pavé*. This yellow-flowered plant we picked and brought home to make a refreshing drink.

We dug into the sides of arroyos and made camps and the older ones told us stories. We gathered *tunas*—the juicy fruit of the prickly pear cactus. We rolled them in the dirt to get rid of their spines, then peeled and ate them.

At night the stars pulsed with light as the constellations rolled across the sky. City lights were far away.

I could sing at the top of my lungs and not disturb anyone except the coyotes.

I had the good fortune to be the eighth child and the first to be born in the hospital. When my mother woke up to see the nurses, who were nuns in white habits, smiling at her, she was frightened--thinking that she was dead and that they were angels.

When the wind blew and it was dark and cold outside, it was hard to get up and go to the outhouse. We kept coffee cans available for such emergencies.

Later on I insisted to my unbelieving English teacher (who told stories about medieval life), that we were very poor, but we also had canopies. The only difference was — the canopies she spoke about went over the beds and our can o'pees — went under the beds.

If we were late getting home there was no room on the two beds — we were grateful for an old blanket on the floor.

Outwardly we showed respect for my father, although he did very little for us. As soon as we could walk, he brought us to the fields to pick onions or cotton. He wouldn't always stay — but picked us up and collected our wages. He did enjoy going to the bar with his friends and smoking Camel cigarettes. My mother was always the fastest picker even if she was usually pregnant. She gave birth to eighteen of us.

Beans and tortillas, along with *chile* and onions were what we ate and if we didn't get there at meal time it was all gone. But, those were the best beans and the softest, most delicious tortillas that my mother could put together. At school even our friends wanted to trade their bologna sandwiches for our burritos.

Sometimes we would have a creamy wheat cereal for breakfast. Flies liked to land and stick in it. We referred to these dark spots in the cereal as volunteer raisins.

We learned to forage in the ditches, picking *quelites*—a weed somewhat like spinach. We knew where sugar cane grew tall and sweet. From the desert we brought *nopales*—the tender prickly-pear pads that we knocked down with sticks. The more adventurous ones gathered vegetables and fruits from surrounding farms, risking buckshot and running so fast their hearts would hurt. My mother never asked where the food came from. She was pleased to add it to our meals.

We knew when the watermelons would be ripe. My father liked nothing better than to sit back and eat a whole watermelon. If we brought him one, we might be rewarded with a smile.

My mother was as lively as my father was quiet. She had a way of laughing at just about everything. She had nicknames for everyone in the neighborhood. A lady who always arrived first with the latest gossip was known as "The Newspaper". *El Mariachi* traveled with his guitar. There was *Chato, Sordo, La Chiva, El Sordo.* My aunt "Sugar" was known for her sour comments.

Even though she had only gone to the third grade she was very sharp and quick-witted. She stitched shirts for us from the flour sacks, turning the Globe mills insignia to the inside or an inconspicuous location. Later on in the sixties, we laughed to see this become a chic style.

My mother had a variety of home remedies and for the most part they worked well. If we got a cut she would sprinkle white flour. It stopped the bleeding and didn't leave a scar.

If we had a cough or cold, we gargled salt water. Then, we got a lemon to suck on. She made a paste out of Vicks vapor rub and flour and lard and at night applied this to our chest and feet. We always felt better in the morning.

One morning I awoke in pain. I was holding onto my ear and crying.

"What's wrong, son?" My mother saw I was hurting.

"My ear! My ear! It hurts—really bad."

"Here, sit in this chair. I will fix it." She sat me down in the kitchen and looked around for paper. She sent my sister next door for a section of the newspaper. I waited, pulling at my ear and wondering what she was going to do. My sister soon returned with a piece of newspaper. I watched my mother roll it into a huge cone. She showed me how to hold the small end in my aching ear while she looked in the cupboard. When she found the matches she lit the wide end of the cone that was away from my head.

I was frightened to see the flames and smoke rise above me.

"You'll be okay. You'll see." She held it in place.

I felt the warmth penetrating inside my ear and the pressure easing. I relaxed as much as I could with a flaming cone above me. I did fear my hair might catch fire.

When the cone had burned down closer to my head she took it away and dunked it in a bucket of water.

"How is the earache?"

"It's gone, now. It doesn't hurt anymore."

And I *did* feel much better. I'm not sure whether it was due to the treatment or the fear of it.

We went barefoot—developing thick calluses on the bottom of our feet. When it was time for school, my mother would borrow a pencil and paper and draw the outlines of our feet. She would go downtown on the bus and come back with a bag of shoes. Then, she brought them out and matched them to us so we would have a pair that fit. One pair of shoes was allowed—they were called *mata viboras* (snake killers), and we hoped our feet would not grow too much unless we could find someone to trade with. We walked about a mile to school, carrying our shoes until we were very close before putting them on, then stepping uncomfortably, but proudly.

Although we usually ate beans, sometimes when there was a little money we would have eggs and my father loved them. Mr. Jackson had a farm nearby and he would sell us the cracked eggs at the price of three dozen for a dollar. The events one Sunday morning stand out vividly in my memory although I don't think I will ever clearly understand them.

That morning my father awoke without too bad of a hangover and a little change in his pocket. And he was hungry for eggs. He called aside my older brother Marco, who was about twelve at the time—four years older than myself—and gave him a dollar and sent him for the eggs. It was about a half a mile away to the farm and we waited eagerly. My mother kept putting wood into the stove to keep it hot as we sat around imagining the taste of fresh eggs.

An hour elapsed and he didn't show up with the eggs. My father grew impatient. He got up from the table and banged his coffee cup down. He stared at me and said, "Go and see what's holding him up."

Quickly, I stood and ran out the door and off to the farm.

As I came closer I saw a police car parked in front of the chicken farm. The door to the building was open. Men in uniforms held Marco with his hands cuffed behind him inside the kitchen.

Somehow, Mr. Jackson claimed, he had reached inside the cash drawer and helped himself to a twenty. He was caught red-handed. When he saw me, Mr. Jackson came up to me and gave me a dollar and told me that it belonged to my brother. Meanwhile they took Marco outside and put him into the police car. As they shut the door, he sent me a piercing look—like a call for help.

"He won't talk. Won't say where he lives. They're taking him away to the juvenile home," Mr. Jackson said, shaking his head.

I was very frightened and ran back home as fast as I could. I slammed the door wide open and screamed, "Hey, the police took my brother! They took him away.... to juvenile home!"

My father looked up and saw my empty arms and asked, "*And where are my eggs?*"

2

As I got older I had plenty of opportunity to see other fathers at work, playing ball or wrestling with their sons, cheering them on, taking time for them. I desperately wanted my father to give me positive attention of any kind. I tried to work on him, in every way, to win his favor. I collected returnable soda bottles to get enough to buy a carton of cigarettes for him for Father's Day—but he took it as just his due as king of the house.

Once I was hopping about, talking and laughing, hoping he would pay attention to me. I don't know what I did that annoyed him, but he picked up his shoe and threw it at me. I dodged just in time. I heard a scream behind me. It hit my mother in the mouth and her lip was bleeding and a tooth was loose. I felt horrified! Now, it became my fault. I was blamed for my mother's tooth that fell out.

Nothing made him change. I started to question whether he really was my father. He was not like me at all.

My mother tried to take care of us as well as she could but I'm sure she was frustrated with so little to give in material things. One summer afternoon the bell of the ice-cream vendor was dinging loudly through the neighborhood and kids were gathering. I was very hungry for ice cream and even though I knew better I asked my mother, "Ma, can I have a dime for ice cream?"

"No, you know there isn't any."

"Please, Ma!" I pleaded and squirmed.

"Go ask your father."

"You know he's gone and he wouldn't give me a thing, even if he were here." I was not happy.

"Well then, go ask the ice cream man. He's your father." She joked.

I was surprised by the thought but I had nothing to lose. I ran after the ice cream truck, yelling, "*Papá! Papá!*"

When I came near, a smiling man turned to me from inside the truck. "*Vente, m' hijo, vente.*"

This was too good to be true. He was happy to hear me and so nice!

"*Qué quieres, hijo?*"

"*Papá, quiero nieve.*"

"*Sí, hijo, sí.*"

Here he was, asking me what I wanted, glad to be called Daddy. He handed me an ice cream cone and didn't ask for any money. I couldn't believe my luck!

That whole summer and the next, when I heard the bell of the ice cream wagon I would go running, shouting "*Papá! Papá!*"

That man never turned me down, and always called me "son".

There was one time when I went after him, calling, "*Papá!*" and too late I saw my father looming in the doorway. He was a dark storm waiting to explode. His eyes glared at me with fire. I was frightened, but the lure of the ice cream was stronger.

I stopped calling out but still ran after the ice cream man and got my treat. Then, I ran up into the desert hills behind our house, hoping that he was too lazy to come after me. I waited behind a mesquite bush until I saw his car leave a dust trail on the road before I slunk home. That night he was too drunk to do anything but fall asleep. His anger fizzled. I was much more cautious after that.

Some of my friends had television sets and occasionally I could watch TV with them. I realized most fathers were not like mine. My favorite TV fathers were on "Father Knows Best" and "Leave It To Beaver". These men talked to their children and did many things with them and for them.

With those examples I soon developed an "imaginary father". He was wonderful! He took me to the movies, played games with me, listened and gave me advice, cheered me on from the stands when I ran track. With the right imagination, the sky was the limit. I could always count on my "imaginary father". He understood. Thanks to him I survived many situations.

I considered telling Dr. Welch about this father, but decided that for now, saying nothing was a safer route.

3

Dr. Welch scratched his scalp and smiled a smile that radiated ice.

"Simon, if you want to get out of here and go home, you must talk to me. I've put in a request to speak to your parents but I haven't heard from them. We have no phone number for you. What *is* your phone number?"

I stared at the wisps of hair that stood up on the back of his head and slowly shook my head.

"You don't know it?"

I didn't move.

"You don't have one?"

I nodded slowly, keeping my eyes on him. I knew he wanted to dissect me and control me. While he was analyzing me, I was studying him. What made *him* tick? He didn't seem very happy, but he *really* wanted me to talk. What did he hope to get from me? On his desk was a picture of his family — his wife and a boy and a girl. The boy was in a baseball uniform and cap. I wanted to ask if he ever had time to go to his games.

I didn't want to tell him anything. I had the ability to recall funny stories and amuse myself and others in all kinds of situations. *My phone?*

I thought back to a time when a man and a woman came running across the yard to the door of our little home. Their only language was English.

"May we borrow your phone, please?"

It was obvious to anyone that cared to look that no overhead lines went into our house — not even those carrying electricity. My brother Marco stood in the doorway as they stared inside. At first he didn't answer. I admired the way he could remain silent and expressionless in a surprising situation. Then he opened the door slightly wider and pointed to the side of the house.

"Our phone booth is over there."

The woman, followed closely by the man, ran over to the outhouse and pulled on the wooden door handle. She actually went inside! Now we poured out of our house — at least ten of us watching her as she came out with her face scrunched up in disgust. We doubled over with laughter as the man shook his fist at us and then they went back to get in their blue car. Even the memory made me shake with laughter inside and I did not hold back a small smile.

4

"What are you thinking about?"

I had forgotten where I was. I looked up at the man across the desk from me and controlled my face — trying to retain a blank expression. I could see that my failure to talk annoyed him. He was picking and poking, trying to get my reaction.

"Okay, can you tell me about school?" He lifted his pencil high in the air and I saw that he kept his fingernails short and very clean.

I could tell he wasn't really interested in my life — was just doing his job. Why should I talk to him at all? Again, in my mind I went back to earlier days. A parade of memories rolled through.

When I started first grade there were eight of us of school age at the time. We walked together. It was about a mile away. Every morning the train whistled and its sound and heavy rumble told us it was seven-thirty. We would start out.

My oldest sister led, the rest of us following, kicking cans, carrying our shoes over our shoulders to make sure they wouldn't wear out and praying that our feet wouldn't grow. We would gather at a little hill close to the school and put on our shoes and Martha tied them and brushed off our dust.

On the way to school we passed a fascinating drug store. Through the large glass windows we stared at a wonderland of goodies—shelves of candy and a soda fountain. All of us really loved anything sweet, since we never had desserts at home. Occasionally we would file into the store, staring at the candy and someone would grab a piece and we would all run the rest of the way. We would share the candy.

The store owner didn't go after us but devised a system that pleased us all. We were each given a specially colored shoe lace to wear and when the storekeepers saw it they would give us a free piece of candy. If there was someone working who didn't know about the arrangement we would point to our shoe.

They would say, "The Mexicans are coming!"

Was it pity, practicality, or extortion, I can't say, but we were glad for the candy!

In my experience, it wasn't always the Anglo people that were the most judgmental. I would no sooner enter the school than the janitor, Victoria, would grab me and pull me aside, poking through my hair, "*A ver, a ver!*" (Let's see!), and in front of others would try to dress me in clothes from the charity box. Later, my friends would ask, "What was she doing?"

"Looking for cooties. She doesn't know they are our friends." I tried to make it a joke.

Victoria knew better than to bully my older siblings but she would pick on others close to my situation and yell at us to get out of the hallway. Sometimes she'd give us a half-tube of toothpaste and tell us to go brush while turning up her nose.

It still makes me mad to think of the superior manner in which she treated us and I would like to whack her one.

If I could get by that dragon lady I would run outside to the merry-go-round and all of us would ride as fast as we could until the second grade teacher came out and hit at us with her umbrella until we would go in.

We were warned not to speak in Spanish or we would be slapped on the hand with a ruler.

My first grade teacher, Miss Penny, was young and beautiful and everyone in the class had a crush on her. She was very kind and this was just her second year teaching. She hadn't been worn down by having my brothers and sisters in class and I wanted to please her; I knew she liked me. I would sit in my desk and smile at her and try very hard to understand her English.

It was entirely different in the next grades. The teachers had worked and worked with my brothers and sisters and had very poor success. They were seen as uncooperative and a waste of time.

When they found out my last name they'd decide: "He's one of those Palomars. He's not going to learn anything. Just give him a comic book and put him in the corner."

Any swats given by the principal were just a joke to us. We didn't blink, just grinned, thanks to my father's education.

But I wanted to learn. I listened to the teachers and tried to behave. A dollar was collected at the beginning of the year for school supplies and since there was no money we didn't pay it. The teacher usually had a box of broken crayons and pieces of pencils for us.

I was in the fourth grade when a teacher started to read *Huckleberry Finn*. Finally, there was a story I really enjoyed!

My parents never went to the school and there was no way for anyone to call home. The only problem came when siblings would tell on you, and that they would do, just to see someone else get in trouble.

It was easy to get hooked on smoking. My father smoked...lots of adults smoked. My grandmother on my mother's side smoked big cigars that we helped roll for her. She was pretty old with long white hair that my mother brushed and braided in the morning sun. No one explained how addictive and killing to the body it is.

A kindly janitor that sometimes pulled me into his closet to see if some clothes would fit—in a nice way, not condescending but happy for me if he could find something—was the one who first gave me a lit cigarette. I took in a deep breath and choked, spitting it out, but it triggered something that made me relax. Everyone who smoked looked like big shots when I was seven. I was soon gathering the butts of cigarettes from the ground and saving them for later. Matches were free and I knew how to light them. No one told me to stop.

Until I started to earn money for myself I could find a soda bottle thrown along a road or in the desert and take it to the tiny store in the neighborhood to turn it in for two cents. With that, if I didn't want candy, I could get one cigarette. I was very young but there were few rules back then. For three cents I could get two cigarettes.

Those free matches made it possible for us to play with fire, too. My friend Ollie and I were behind my house lighting little things on fire, sticks and paper. Then he lit a broken plastic water gun that had been lying in the ground. To our surprise it flamed up with a hot yellow spurt of fire and black smoke. Ollie kicked it and it went flying toward me. It stuck to my face — near my eye, and I screamed. Instinctively, I lay down on the ground and threw sand and dirt on my face. Ollie yelled for help. It hurt so bad! I couldn't see out of my left eye.

Usually, if we got cut my mother would throw flour on the wound and it would stop bleeding and heal. But this was much different. They took me to a doctor. I don't remember how I got there. He cleaned it out and examined my eye and told me I was lucky that I was going to be able to see out of it and to never, ever play with fire again. On one spot on my forehead my skin was raw, red and shriveled, He applied a white cream that made it feel better and told my mother that she would have to clean it and apply that cream for a long time.

When I went back to school the nurse took over that job. I would sit in her office in the morning until she had time to clean my forehead and apply the cream. It didn't look bad during the first part of the day but by lunchtime it turned yellow and oozy.

I discovered that my horrible appearance provided some advantages. When I sat near some people that were eating they might look up at me and lose their appetite. Then I would lean towards them and say, "Are you going to eat that?" A lot of times they shook their heads, clutched at their stomachs and left the table. That led to a lot of free food and desserts.

I guess I learned a lot of things the hard way. I found one can almost always find some advantage in any situation, however bad it seems at first.

It was school policy to advance students after two years, whether they had learned anything or not and I soon was gaining in grade on the others. I remember that when I was in the third grade, my sister Maggie, who was six years older, was in the sixth grade. She was much more interested in the boys than in learning anything. She had very beautifully carved her initials plus a boy's, enclosed in a heart, into a school desk. This caused a lot of trouble. She was accused of destroying school property and a note was sent home, demanding twenty dollars to pay for the damage. Of course, my parents couldn't or wouldn't pay for it and at that point her formal education was finished.

None of my older brothers or sisters went beyond seventh grade, except my sister Vela, who was tickled pink to ride the bus, a new experience for eighth grade. She would get ready—carrying her folder in her hand, get on the bus and wave, smiling from the window. However, she never made it to class, but would hide out in the restrooms until lunch.

Living without basic things was harder for us because at that time everyone else had plumbing and electricity. But, if we felt bad we would think of those on the other side of the border. We bought kerosene for our lamp at five cents a quart and we never had any need to lock our doors.

If you are close to the South Pole almost every direction is north. So, if you don't feel sorry for yourself, when you are close to the bottom, almost every path leads upwards.

Sometimes, in the dark, a knock would sound on our door and my mother would get up, no matter what the hour, and fix a meal. I don't know how they recognized the house, or if we were on some immigrant underground railway, but my mother never turned anyone away, even if there was almost nothing in the house.

I know poverty can be a state of mind or a matter of comparison.

5

Dr. Welch, in his tidy white uniform, would never be able to understand.

We had been drilled from an early age:

"Don't tell! Do you want the welfare to come and take you away?"

This fear was enough to keep us quiet. He was intent on getting into my head, but imagination was an area in which I was always very rich. When I came into his office and he drilled me with leading questions, the memories would swirl and swarm into my brain and run like fish up a stream. I would put my arms behind my head and lean back, smiling at him. Each question would set off a story. But these he could not hear.

"What about holidays?" He tapped his fingers on the desk.

Easter? We cleaned graves and gathered at the cemetery. For us it was not a time of candy baskets but a time of resurrection...the spirits came up from the graves. The earth gave up treasures. We searched for gold that the Spanish explorers buried in the mountains. Although we did not find gold we always had the hope that it was there... somewhere.

I liked to climb in the Franklin Mountains with my friends. We would go to a spring known as *El Ojito de Agua*. Nearby, we found caves to explore. One of them was used by a very old man who tended his small goatherd. He made a tasty cheese from their milk. The only drawback was his hands were always very dirty.

Halloween — now that was fun!

One thing everyone in my family agreed upon was the fact that sugar is wonderful in all its forms! A sack of sugar was very cheap when I was growing up. From a very young age we drank coffee — it was also very cheap. Morning coffee for most of us was almost drowned in sugar.

But there was one time of the year when we could actually get a lot of sweets. It was also a day when mischief was allowed and not punished. It was a wonderful day! We waited and planned for Halloween.

If we were at school we squirmed and wiggled until the last bell rang and then raced home as fast as we could.

Costumes were simple — a little black soot on the face for the boys — maybe a mustache. The girls wore makeup and earrings and the rags they already wore turned them into gypsies.

We had to hurry because there was a definite time element to success.

Halloween isn't celebrated the same way across the border in Juarez. While we just had to get ready and run to a good area, where rich people lived, other children planned to stay with their El Paso relatives or came across in truckloads, even before dark. Whole families drove across to trick-or-treat. Even an occasional grandmother would show up at someone's door...maybe carrying a baby and smiling a pumpkin smile..."Treek treat!" They would begin before dark and go until all the goodies were gone and the lights turned off. There were also the bag-snatchers — those too big or too embarrassed to go to the door but who wanted their share.

My brothers and sisters and I didn't care how big we grew — this was the golden-sweet opportunity to satisfy that craving and stock up for the rest of the year.

I remember one Halloween that stood out among the rest. We started out before dark, with pillowcases in hand, laughing and running in a group towards the country club area where rich people bought chocolate bars and other candy of all kinds. We sprinted between houses and did quite well, munching as we ran.

Soon it grew dark and some houses had turned off their lights. My brother Marco was annoyed by such houses and saved cherry bombs from the Fourth of July. They were a nickel back then. We had spread out but stayed within earshot for safety from the snatchers. I was at the door of one house when a loud boom went off further down the street. The man that answered the door looked out into the dark as he distributed candy.

"What was that?" He worried.

As we worked our way along the street we saw some mailboxes blown apart. Another group of trick-or-treaters grew frightened.

"Who's doing that?"

"It's just my brother." I wanted to answer but at the age of seven, I knew better.

My brother Marco had lived with my grandparents until they died. Others had told me how that grandfather would put on his Mexican revolutionary war uniform, take out his *carabina*, get on his horse with his rifle at his shoulder and ride up the street. He had fought with Pancho Villa, as did my cigar-smoking grandmother. Marco was not afraid of anything but liked to live a little dangerously himself.

As we tired and started to drag our pillowslips down our street, eating candy as we went a voice came out of the blackness, "*Ayúdame!, Socorro!!*"

This was close to our house. *What had happened?*

"That sounds like our neighbor, Magdalena. She must be in trouble," my sister said, as we hurried into the back yard.

"Help! I can't get out." It was a muffled sound near the ground.

"Oh no! Somebody knocked over her outhouse and I think she was using it!" I often saw Magdalena walking along the street with her cane.

"Hold on, Magdalena, we're going to shift it so the door will open."

"Ooooh," was the pained reply. "I'm going to get whoever did this!"

Together we rocked the wooden frame until the wall with the door attached rolled sideways and the door could swing free. We helped her to come out and regain her feet.

"Don't worry, we'll find out who it was," said my brother, with a straight face as he held her arm and walked her to her door.

And then we were at our own house, smaller than a garage, lit only by a kerosene lamp, with the front door hanging by a hinge and the windows covered with old blankets, nothing but sand and another outhouse in the yard. It looked appropriate for Halloween décor.

We went inside and spread out our candy, admiring our stash and depleting it at the same time—trading for favorite flavors—hurrying because there was always the chance someone else would get it.

Suddenly, someone rapped at our door. No one we knew ever knocked at our unlocked door. We froze. When the sound was repeated, my oldest sister cracked open the door and we all peeked out with curiosity.

"Trick or treat!" Two little blond boys nicely costumed as Superman and Roy Rogers held out their bags very politely.

"*Qué*?" We couldn't believe it. Nobody had ever and I mean ever come to our door to trick-or-treat. They stood and looked at us expectantly.

"Trick or treat." They waited with outstretched bags. I'm sure they could see the candy strewn on our floor inside. But, we felt we had worked hard to earn it.

All at once we looked at each other and burst into laughter and pointed at them. They just stood there, although we made fun of them. We didn't know how to act and laughed to cover our own embarrassment. Then, one left with his head down, and then the other. We closed the door and ate our candy. This was ever after remembered as the one and only Halloween we had trick-or-treaters.

6

School life held all kinds of surprises. My fourth grade year had barely begun when first thing in the morning I got a note to go to the principal's office. What did Mrs. McPherson want now?

"Simon, I wonder if you would be interested in a proposition?" She bent down, studying my face, and tilted her head.

A proposition? What was that? It didn't sound good. By the fourth grade I had learned to be wary.

I gave her my practiced, steady smile, and said nothing.

"The cooks and kitchen staff need a little help. We could make an arrangement so that if you assisted them in washing dishes every day after lunch—well, you wouldn't have to pay for your lunch."

Now, she really had my attention. The school lunch was often very good—tacos and enchiladas—and even a dessert! I never had money to buy it and so just pretended I didn't want it. That September I was always hungry.

"Yes." I replied without changing my expression.

"Good, then, I will send home a slip asking for your parent's permission."

"Okay, then." I stood stiffly and left, hardly believing my luck.

That slip was signed by my mother's forged signature before it ever reached home to be lost or torn. I would carefully turn it in the next day so it would not be so obvious. At home, often my mother was too busy or there was no pen or pencil available. We all found it easier to sign her name ourselves and she didn't mind. At school no one mentioned that she had many different-looking signatures.

The next day, Ramona, the cook's assistant, made me sit down to a plate that was the envy of all. I ate slowly, relishing every delicious bite. Then, she showed me how to scrape and rinse the lunch dishes and put them into the large dishwasher. I worked carefully and felt important as part of the kitchen crew. The ladies were always joking and laughing as they worked and spoke nicely to me. They gave me extra portions.

"Can I have some of that?"

"No, that's for Simon; he's helping out."

"Aaw!"

It was a great feeling to be the object of envy. That fall and winter I sat to eat lunch among my friends, then, went to work in the kitchen, missing recess — but not minding at all.

When spring came around — so did my birthday. It was usually just like any other day at home. I never had a birthday cake before, much less a party. I would be lucky if someone even remembered to tell me, "Happy Birthday!"

I remember *this* day. After I had eaten lunch I got up to go work. Then, Ramona came out and told me, "No, never mind. Today, you don't work. You don't have to do a thing!"

The kitchen crew soon surrounded me and before I knew it they brought out a cupcake with a lighted candle and everyone sang, "Happy Birthday".

I struggled to keep my face straight but inside I was crumbling apart and my eyes were brimming with water. I felt like crying—but no, I couldn't let myself, not here in front of everyone! My first birthday cake!

7
Christmas

When Christmas approached a sense of excitement filled the hallways and classes of our schools like a maddening perfume. Usually, every classroom had a small tree and some were lighted. For me it was a time of hope and of disappointment. No matter how good or bad I was through the year there would be no gift-wrapped toy for me or any of my many brothers and sister. The closest I would get would be helping my friends wrap presents – and this I enjoyed. I became an expert – cutting the paper to size, folding and taping the edges precisely. I found out what others were getting and I would later come to their houses to play.

Then there was the Christmas exchange – drawing names in the classroom. For us this was difficult when we had little to give. My seventh grade class comes to mind. Mr. Garner was our teacher and he was a good teacher, but in a reflexive reaction to his hand on my shoulder I had punched him in the stomach early in the year and that caused a lot of trouble.

I drew the name of a girl, Celia—a friendly quiet girl with long black hair. I knew that if I were to give her something I would have to work extra hard—some place other that the fields where my family already labored. I arranged to mow lawns and weed for an older lady who was very understanding. Then, I decided on a bottle of sweet perfume as her gift—hoping it would be acceptable.

I worked hard and was soon wrapping it with paper and tape at a friend's. Anything I left at home had a good chance of disappearing.

"Do you think she'll like it?" I worried.

"She'll love it!" He nodded.

"Do you know who has my name?"

"No, I haven't heard anything at all."

The big day before the holidays arrived and we distributed the presents from under the class tree. Celia slowly unwrapped her present then turned and smiled at me. I smiled in return.

Then very, very, slowly, savoring every moment, I removed the ribbon from the narrow blue box that was given to me. I read the tag. Oh no! It was from Mr. Garner—I didn't deserve a thing from him after what I had done. I sat up straight in my desk and took the top off the box. Inside was a beautiful shiny pen-and-pencil set along with a nice handkerchief. I was overwhelmed. I could hardly lift my head to look at him—but I will be grateful forever for his kindness. I resolved to be an angel the rest of the year.

The teachers knew we barely had clothes. No parent ever came to school; we only had supplies we could find discarded or borrowed from other kids. But every year in all the classrooms the teachers would ask, "Who doesn't have a tree at home?" We would lie. Who wants to look bad in front one's classmates?......but *they knew*.

So, because they didn't take into account there were seven of us in the elementary one year, when school let out for Christmas vacation, we got home to find our teachers each had brought us the class tree.

My mother just laughed. There was no way to fit them inside. They were pretty but we had no electricity to display the lights. She had made a giant pot of *menudo* that day and she invited them in for a bowl. Not one of the teachers stayed to eat though her *menudo* is the very best. *I wouldn't mind having a big bowl today!* Sometimes she flavored it with so much red chili it was painful. I think she figured if we could stand it, it would toughen us for the rest of life's aches and disappointments.

There is one present we did get to unwrap every Christmas. We always knew what it was—we just didn't know the color. For years my aunt worked for a clothing manufacturing plant and could get some real bargains. She spent hours wrapping and on Christmas day each of her children and many nieces and nephew would open a package. Suddenly there would appear 30 or more children in an identical plaid flannel shirt or skirt—all red one year—blue or green the next—roaming the neighborhood! They were new and soft and we thanked her.... but, it was never a toy.

8

Culebra

It had been a day of howling winds. In the evening thick, dark clouds streamed in from the east. Large black thunderclouds curled above the mountain. My mother insisted we cover the mirror with a sheet in case lightning came. The temperature dropped quickly and that night I was happy to hide under the blankets. I liked to tell people that I slept between eight and six — my brother was eight and my sister was six.

Our tiny adobe home sat on a sandy lot and the streets were dirt. If the rains were heavy and continuous, it could all turn to mud. My mother feared this kind of deluge.

Usually, a good rain was very welcome. During the hot summer a shower drew us out of the house to play in the arroyos and drink in the fragrance of the creosote bushes. But, when it rained and rained, streams would overflow from all the water running from the mountains. Small children were sometimes swept under if they were not careful. Across the river it was worse. In Juarez whole hillsides could slide.

That night thunder boomed and rolled; lightning sizzled and lit the sky and hit nearby. I had seen what it could do — many of the giant cottonwoods along the river were split. The thunder continued to rock us. This storm was not moving on. The black clouds hung low. My father was not home. My mother was frowning. She did not light the kerosene lantern. The lightning was the only source of light. While she worried, I went to sleep.

All of a sudden my blankets were ripped off of me.

"Get up."

"What?" I was very sleepy.

"*You* have to do it!"

"What are you talking about?"

"Come, you'll see." She dragged me into the kitchen. From somewhere she pulled out a large machete and held it with the blade in the air. A flash of lightning close by showed me how large and sharp it was. I was nine years old and had nothing on but my underwear.

"You have to cut it!" She opened the back door and I could see the pitch black sky.

"Cut what?'

"*La culebra*! Cut the snake in the sky — like this!" She raised the machete and cut into the air repeatedly, then put it into my hands.

"Yes! That's right. Straight up then turn and twist into its heart. Make circles."

In the yard she had scattered the ashes from the stove into a ring.

"Stay in the middle. Go!" She shoved me out the door into the lightning and pouring rain.

I was shivering and frightened — especially when lightning struck nearby, but I stabbed and swirled the knife into the sky with all my strength. I was even more frightened of my mother's strange intense dread. It seemed like I was out there for hours.

Why I was picked to do this — I don't know. Maybe I was the most expendable. Maybe I was the one willing. Her mother was born in a cave in the mountains of Chihuahua, but what kind of a ritual was this? Was I supposed to be some kind of native sacrificial offering? She never told me. I jumped when lightning flashed and the thunder shook the ground. I just wanted it all to end.

Eventually the clouds began to break up and the storm moved away. At last I was allowed back inside!

Later, in school, I learned how lightning is attracted to metal and conducts electricity. I was spared that night and I am glad!

9

Rabbits

My father acquired a rifle which he kept hidden in the *ropero*—an upright cabinet that acted as a closet. He liked to go with his friends into the desert and shoot at cans or jackrabbits. Sometimes he would bring home the rabbits and my mother would skin and clean them and put them into a large pot with wild herbs and onions and garlic and potatoes if she had them. I loved rabbit stew. My father occasionally took along my oldest brother, Ricardo, his namesake, when his friends brought their sons. Neither one was a very good shot but my other brothers and I wished we were invited. This never happened.

When he left to go elsewhere, we would watch the dust of his car settle back onto the road and we would get into that *ropero*. We snuck out into the desert as far as we could and practiced our shooting. It wasn't long before we could shoot a jackrabbit as it bounded out from a hole. Someone had given my younger brother, Nate, a nice dog that was part German shepherd and when we took him with us, that dog was great at flushing out the rabbits.

If we came back with a rabbit my mother would tell us to skin it and would quickly put it into the pot. She didn't ask where we had been or if we took the rifle. We were careful to know when my father was coming and would have the gun back in place before he drove up.

After a while we found strange lumpy growths on the meat after they were skinned. My mother said they had some disease and it was probably not good to eat them anymore.

She had friends that lived further out in the country. When someone would drive her, she loved to go visit with them. She and Edna had been friends all their lives. Edna was married with quite a few children—of course, not as many as we had. She and her husband had several acres of land. They had chickens and goats. They also had a hutch in which they raised rabbits for food. These were plump white cottontails and they were pretty easy to take care of.

One day my mother came back with a pair of them. My brothers and I were set to work digging out a large, wide hole at least two feet deep that ran next to the back of our house. We laid down chicken wire on the bottom and built up the sides and walls. We covered it and made a little hinged door out of chicken wire and two by fours.

Everyone wanted to pet the rabbits. Pretty soon baby rabbits appeared, hopping about. We gathered greens to poke inside the cage. The farmers would sell us alfalfa dust in gunny sacks for a quarter. The rabbits relished this and kept multiplying.

One of my sisters loved to sit inside the cage and pet the rabbits. Vela never brought them food or cleaned the cage but would sit on the ground and grab whichever rabbit was near and stroke their soft fur with a dreamy smile on her face. She would hold the rabbit next to her cheek, leaning her head towards it.

The rabbits dug hole after hole and made nests underground. We had to be careful while stepping inside the cage. If you didn't watch out your foot would sink into a hole and baby rabbits could be crushed.

We ate rabbit on a regular basis. It tastes a lot like chicken. When my mother asked us for some we would conk the rabbits on the head, then clip them by the ears onto the clothes line and clean them out. My sister would howl. But, none of us turned down my mother's rabbit stew.

It didn't take long for the rabbit population to really take off. One day we saw something moving the dirt on our floor. It looked like a nose but we didn't know if it was a rat or a rabbit until it emerged. To our surprise the rabbits began to pop up inside our house. They couldn't go through the chicken wire but they dug beneath the foundation walls of our house and on inside. My little brothers would squeal and try to catch them. The rabbits were quick enough to dive back into their burrows.

Our dirt floor became more and more dangerous. You could step in a hole just about anywhere. It wasn't long after this that our neighbor, Mr. Montes, visited and started urging my father that it was time for our house to have some cement on the floor.

My father had no ambition to fix anything—it was the neighbor man, Eduardo Montes, who convinced him to put cement over our dirt floor and pretty much forced him to help. We watched our indoor dirt playground disappear. Then, there was no more making roads for a stick car or digging a little hole if you didn't want to go to the outhouse in the cold.

10

Another Egg Story

Our neighborhood was small. Many of the adults had come across the river during the unsettling Mexican Revolution and everyone knew everyone else. We were often sent on errands to borrow from a neighbor or assist someone. Neighbors were closer than the small store and there were few cars parked in the dusty streets. People made do with what they had.

The women that were married were very protective of their man. They didn't want him to wander. It didn't matter if he was 70 years old; every woman knew a man was weak and the women were fierce in defense of their property. Sometimes this could cause problems, especially around those with a leaning towards mischief, and my brother Marco was such a one.

He was living up the street from the rest of us in a tiny adobe home with our Grandma Olivia, who was single. She expected him to help out, chop the wood for the cook stove, etc., but he wasn't very enthusiastic about any of it. This afternoon she was cooking and the stove was hot. She wasn't about to leave it.

"Marco, *hijo*, (Every male was *hijo*)... run over and bring me some eggs from *Doña* Colacha. She will give me some."

Now Marco was not very willing to go but didn't want to openly defy his Grandma. He hesitated a minute then looked out to the street and said with a very serious expression, "Didn't you know? Doña Colacha died this morning."

"*Qué?*" She stared into his face. He didn't blink. "*Seguro?*"

"*Sí, Abuelita*, I am very sure."

"Ay, Dios!" she wailed, tearing off her apron and forgetting her cooking.

"*Se murió Doña Colacha!*" she yelled out to her neighbors.

"Ay. *Como?*"

"I don't know what happened to her. She wasn't young."

Neighborhood voices worked better than telephones. At once there appeared a small group of women hurrying out of their houses, and moving down the street to *Doña* Colacha's home, chattering as they went.

Now *Doña* Colacha did have a husband of 40 some years and he was in his t-shirt, resting on an old mattress in the shade of a mulberry tree as was the custom. Don Pedro sat up when he saw the women coming....surprised to see them come directly to him.

They surrounded him, hugging him and crying. "*Lo siento!* I am so sorry to hear!" they wailed, almost smothering him with embraces.

He didn't know what it was about but he was thoroughly enjoying such female attention. They made a huge commotion under the tree.

44

Pretty soon *Doña* Colacha heard all the voices and she came out of the door to see what was going on. What she saw made her furious—Grandma Olivia with Don Pedro's face pressed against her bosom, tears running down her face.

"Leave my man alone!" she yelled.

The women looked up to see her red, familiar face and they screamed as if she was a ghost. Of course, to them, she was a ghost!

"Get away! Is this how you behave?" She picked up a piece of wood and raised it over her head.

And then they began hugging her, too and crying and she couldn't make heads or tails of the situation.

"*Doña* Colacha, is it really you?"

"*Porqué*? Are you crazy?"

"Oh, *graçias a Diós*!"

"Marco told me that you were dead."

"And you believed that boy?"

Marco, who had watched it all from a safe distance, thoroughly enjoying the whole show, knew better than to stick around. He was a fast runner—very fast—but he had to come home sometime.

11

With a tiny home bursting with many children, we had every reason to explore our neighborhood. If we were not taken to work in a field, we had the summer to roam along the river and its irrigation ditches, sampling all the sugar cane, the wild pomegranate and apricot trees that we could find. No one looked for us until evening.

One day I roamed with Lily, one of my older sisters, along a large ditch when I was happy to spot a vine connecting many large green watermelons. My mouth watered at the thought of the red juicy flesh inside and I pulled the biggest one off the plant. I raised it to the height of my waist and let it drop into the sand. It went "thud" but didn't crack. Lily smiled at me and went to sit in the shade of a wild elm. Then I found a rock and dropped the melon on it. It bounced! I kicked at it, then raised it over my head and threw it as hard as I could against the rock. It bounced high, like a ball, then, rolled further away. I looked over at my sister who threw her head back and laughed at me showing her white teeth.

"That's not a watermelon."

"What do you mean?"

"It's a *chilacoyote*."

"What is that?"

"It looks just like a watermelon but the skin is so thick you can hardly break it, even with a knife. They use the inside for the seeds and to make candy. It's too much work and not really sweet. Just leave it there. You were so funny trying to break it!" She broke off a piece of sugarcane growing nearby, peeling a piece before handing it to me.

"Here, Simon, try this."

I chewed on it as we walked toward the big, main ditch that carried water for miles to the farms and orchards, splintering off into many medium and smaller ditches as it went.

We found my older brothers fishing in a wide muddy pool that branched off the fast-flowing main ditch. It was here that the catfish would loll in the muck and they could grab them if they didn't like the bait. Whoever brought home a large catfish would be hailed as a hero. My mother loved catfish or any other fish. She would clean the bones of a carp with her teeth.

I desperately wanted to catch one but I didn't know how to swim. My brothers were willing to teach me, but it wasn't the patient Red-Cross sponsored lessons.

I shed my clothes and waded in. My oldest brother pulled me out into the middle and let go. I was terrified. I sank to the bottom, holding my breath and swinging my arms. The water was way over my head. I pushed up with my legs, and struggling to the surface, gagging on water I had swallowed. Then I went under again. I thought I was going to drown.

Desperately, I started paddling and kicking, and could feel myself moving. I grabbed at some reeds growing along the side and pulled until my head was above water and I was on the side.

"Hey, you can swim now!" My siblings encouraged me, nodding.

With that very elementary instruction I timidly tried to do it again—but where my feet could still touch. Eventually I could paddle with my head above the muddy water and I was not so afraid. This was the standard swimming lesson. I did not drown, so, I could swim!

12

When I was about twelve, Mrs. McDougal considered me big enough and strong enough to try out for night-time field irrigation. No one much liked this job because it was lonesome and hard work. It had to be done at night in order to lessen the water evaporation. The ditch rider would open gates to release water scheduled to come along the canals from the Rio Grande and it was up to the farmers to get it into the fields. The El Paso area averages about 8 inches of rain a year, so, without irrigation, plants in the field die quickly.

At dusk, I headed to the farm, carrying a burrito, a jug of drinking water and a lantern. The thirsty cotton plants were still small and lay in acres and acres of neat rows extending on either side of the ditches.

I had practiced taking the long, curved, irrigation pipes, lowering them into the water to create suction, then, maneuvering them into the rows in a way that would provide a gravity flow. The challenge would be to do it in the dark and keep moving the water evenly throughout the field.

No moon yet. I lit the lantern and set it on the earthen dam next to the ditch. The water was coming through the canal. I laid out one pipe after another and watched the rows fill with water. Wherever there was blockage I took the shovel and moved the dirt. The only noise at first was the gurgling water, clanking pipes and droning mosquitoes. I had to stay alert and not let my imagination wander.

The wind came up and I heard a creaking sound. I tried to shut my mind to the scary stories we were told — *La Llorona,*--the woman who had drowned her own children in the river and was sent out looking for them. *"Mis hijos!"* she would wail over and over. "Where are my children?" *When was the moon going to come up over the Franklin Mountains?* The light from the lantern did not reach far.

All of a sudden I heard low moaning close by. What could that be? I brought the lantern in its direction but could see nothing. Then the wind blew it out. Something near shrieked so loudly my skin crawled. Was it really *La Llorona?* I froze.

I was all by myself and no one could hear me even if I screamed. There was no place to hide.

In the distance car lights were coming. They drew closer then, turned onto the levee toward me. There was a horrible yowling followed by footsteps skittering past me.

To my relief I could see they were just cats. Chuy, the ditch rider, pulled up.

"I just came by to see how you were doing your first night. Is everything all right?"

"Sure. Everything's okay."

"Looks like you are doing a good job. There will be moonlight soon."

"Good!"

In the morning I collected my wages from Mrs. McDougal. She put five dollar bills into my hand and I was proud.

13

There was one activity that we did as a family that we all enjoyed—from the youngest to the oldest and even, my parents. A drive-in-theater was built on the edge of town—about a mile and a half from our neighborhood. Most of the week they showed movies in English but Tuesday night was "Mexican night". Popular Spanish movies—such as those starring Antonio Aguilar, Pedro Infante or Cantinflas, would be shown and wonder of all wonders—it was only a dollar for a carload.

Some of us walked over. The younger ones crammed inside the car with my parents and we met outside the drive-in. Then, we lay across the hood or sat on the bumper as we came to the entrance. We always got our dollar's worth!

Mr. Schulz, the owner, knew us very well. He took us off the outside of the car and showed us through the gate, smiling. He had little toys for each child, straw finger-traps, jacks, or such. He made most of his money by selling popcorn, sodas and hotdogs.

For us, it was a great time to walk around the outside edge; the cars filled the center. There were always a lot of boys and girls my age. Those of us who worked the fields might smell of onions or *chiles*. The girls strolled past in pairs, their long hair swinging, their eyes made up, smiling at the boys who walked in the opposite direction. There was a lot of dreaming and stolen kisses but it was safe. Everyone knew it was not permanent. We might not see the same girls for months, or again at all.

Saturday or Sunday was the usual day scheduled for the once a week bath. When you consider the large number of children and the fact that water had to be carried from next door and heated on a wood stove you realize it was quite a big undertaking. As soon as I was able, I was expected to carry pails of water.

It was much easier in the warm months when the water was already a comfortable temperature! In the winter we chopped wood and brought enough of it inside to keep the stove hot. The pails were heated and dumped into the big tin tub, along with some cooler water. There was no time to soak—several of us at a time would lather quickly with the big, rough bar of soap and when our hair was soapy someone would pour warm water over our heads. We would hop out and shivering, dry with a towel.

If it was morning we looked out across the river at the Juarez Mountains and the bright glow of the sun worked its way down into the valley before it came to us over the Franklins. We welcomed the sunshine and basked in it like lizards before putting on our clothes.

I remembered I must have been about six when a car drove by as we were sunning. I recognized a girl in my class from school. It was Mabel and her brother, Johnny. I was happy to see them and stood up and waved wildly. They waved back with big grins on their faces.

At the time, I thought nothing was unusual about it. It was Mabel who remembered — and then we were in Junior High. That was part of that horrible day! I tried to block it out but I could still hear her voice. Now she was taller than I was and with long sandy-colored hair.

"Hi, Simon."

"Mabel!"

"Remember."

"Remember what?"

"That day we drove by your house," she smiled widely, her friends surrounding her.

I looked at her coldly, hoping she wouldn't say anything else. Junior High was one embarrassment after another.

"The day you stood up and waved at Johnny and me — and you didn't have any clothes on," she giggled. Her friends stared at me and laughed.

Life had taught me that a good attack was the best defense and I had honed my skills. Seldom was I left without a comeback.

"Well, did you like what you saw?" I looked her directly in the eyes, boldly.

She blushed and turned away. I was a little boy when she had looked at me, but now I knew a few more things and hard work had made me strong.

That school day had started out bad and just got worse and worse. If I ever do talk to Dr. Welch I'm sure he'd have some things to think about. He couldn't possibly understand. *How was I going to get out of here?* I knew I had to stay calm. If I showed rage he would force me to take pills.

14

Before she married and had babies, my mother helped lay the foundation stones of the little mission church close by us. It was erected of adobe, gradually — as the people could manage. It had a small bell tower and a wooden floor. There was an outhouse in the back. A Jesuit priest would come on Sunday to say Mass but generally no one was there during the week.

Although each Sunday different priests came, they were all given the respect due their learning and position. They would extend the back of their hand and we were taught to kiss it. Once I saw the priest come from the outhouse to the steps to greet us as we entered and I pulled back from kissing his hand and was therefore, scolded. But I was sure there was no washbasin in the outhouse. I knew he was only human.

We were all baptized as infants and assigned godparents. The older ones were luckier. By the time they got to me there were six of us with the very same godparents.

The church raised money in the fall with a fair that had game booths and enchiladas and *gorditas*. Bingo, cakewalks and raffles were very popular. At Christmas time they held a party for the kids and there were drawings in which some of us would win gifts.

One year we all waited with our friends, our eyes shining with hope. There was only one wrapped present remaining when the man wearing a red elf hat called out, "Guadalupe Perez." We jumped up. Lupe was a boy I often played with, a little younger than myself.

He had won! He ran up to the front to take the present wrapped in green, shiny foil. We followed him and craned our necks over his shoulder as he slowly tore off the ribbon and paper. Inside to everyone's surprise was a blue-eyed doll with long blond hair.

What a mistake! Guadalupe is also a girl's name, the same as one of my sisters. Lupe's mouth turned down as his face reddened. Everyone laughed and some of the older boys hooted. He suddenly burst into tears and threw the doll to the floor. The girls closest to him immediately scrambled and swarmed over to grab for it as he ran out of the door, crying.

Sometimes a very old woman would walk all the way from the area along the Rio Grande called "Naranjo" to instruct us in the catechism. Others would gather us and teach us—rewarding us with candy if we could memorize prayers.

We attended Mass on Sundays and feast days. If we arrived late, all of the scarf-covered heads would swing around to frown at us, rosaries in hand. The Bible was not something we were supposed to read on our own. We were all very aware of sin and hell.

During those years Catholics were not supposed to eat meat on Fridays. We had no electricity so our cooler was a wooden icebox that occasionally held ice. My mother was practical. With so many children and meat seldom on the menu she announced, "If we have meat we are going to eat it." And so we did.

Most all the families in our area were Catholic but there were some who were referred to as "Holy Rollers". We heard that they screamed and tore their hair and rolled around on the ground. So, of course we were very curious to see this.

They met in a stone house on the corner and we would hear music and loud singing. The windows were small and above our heads—too high for gazing through. When I was about 12 a few friends and I decided to sneak in the back door and make fun of them. We slipped in and stood in the back.

Young and old were crowded together, singing to guitar music and the rhythm of a tambourines. Some were raising their hands and jumping. No one seemed to notice our entrance. There was an excitement that was very strange to me. "*Alabanza a Dios*" and "Alleluia" were like a background refrain.

Eloisa, an old, old neighbor with coke-bottle thick glasses suddenly pointed to the ceiling and shrieked, "I can see! I can see!" I felt a chill run through me although it was a sweltering day. Others called out prayers and praises in no particular order.

I didn't see anyone rolling on the ground or tearing their hair. Some were sitting quietly, tears streaming down their cheeks. What was going on? Was this the real presence of the Holy Spirit as some had said? I had come to laugh—but I was not laughing.

A short, mustached man began to speak at the front in a voice that was almost yelling. A call was given to come forward to be saved. This was so different from the orderly, predictable service that I usually attended. Here was fervor and a bit of craziness mixed with joy. My head seemed in a fog.

I don't know how it happened but at the end I found myself in front of the congregation — people surrounding me calling, "Praise to God! He has touched him!"

I am by nature skeptical but this experience stayed with me all my life. And I still have no idea how I got to the front of the room.

The preacher gave me a small Gideon New Testament and I began to read it when I wandered up alone in the hills.

15

"Craaack!" Doctor Welch pounded something metallic onto his desk. I was startled out of my memories.

"I've been trying to talk to you for weeks! You are wasting my time. Your family hasn't been here. Do you like being locked up?" His face reddened as he snapped at me. He stood and flexed his arms.

So, this was the new tactic...provoke me into doing something stupid. I wasn't going to fall for it!

I straightened my back and tensed like a cat watching its prey...not blinking.

He came towards me with outstretched hands. If he touched me, I feared I might swing at him. I decided it was time to speak.

"Hey, I really need to go to the bathroom."

"So, you **can** talk. You speak English." He drew back and went to write something on a paper on his desk. "You'll have to wait until the end of the session," he told me with a smile that looked more like a grimace.

So, I settled back on my stool and started to think about Don Pablo. He had always been friendly and happy.

I got a taste of business wheeling and dealing, while accompanying my neighbor, Don Pablo. He welcomed help from neighborhood kids. He drove an old dark-blue Chevy truck. The running board was permanently bent where he stepped in and out and the whole driver's side of the truck sagged low when he got in. He was a short man and weighed over 350 pounds. It took such an effort for him to move that he seldom got out of the truck. Kids from all over would pile in the back and even hang on the sides to go with him.

He never told anybody to get off and we always had fun. First, we would go to the Gomez farm and haggle with *Señor* Gomez for his produce. Each claimed the other was robbing them.

"It cost something to grow them, you know."

"Oh, you don't have to do anything!"

"How am I going to make it if I sell the watermelons for a nickel? And the tomatoes, you want them for free?" Mr. Gomez threw his arms in the air.

"You know I have to feed my big family."

"You're making money."

Don Pablo was always smiling—his toothless smile—even when they were arguing and I could see Mr. Gomez enjoyed the exchange. They eventually agreed, and although each claimed it was highway robbery, they each got a good deal.

I helped load the back of the truck with watermelons, onions, tomatoes, corn and *chile*, or whatever else was in season and we drove to neighborhoods that lay away from the farmlands. Here there were customers eager to buy. Watermelons went for a quarter or fifty cents and everyone was satisfied. Sometimes they rolled around and split in the truck and I got a piece to eat.

On the way back, Don Pablo's nephew Boomer, who was a bit slow, picked up the mushy tomatoes and threw them at the people along the street. He would shake with laughter if he actually hit a target and they ran charging after the truck. For the rest of us, it was just fun to be riding.

Some days, Don Pablo would fill up an ice chest in the back with sodas and bags of chips and other snacks and we would head to the fields where people were picking cotton or hoeing the rows. He hated to get out of the truck once he had settled in and so I got to do a lot of packing and handing out things for him. He carried an empty tomato can turned upside down and hung alongside him in the truck because it was very hard for him to swing himself out to go to the bathroom.

The men came up and gave him money for cokes and I would get them from the ice chest. We usually stayed quite a while and much of the ice turned to water.

If I am ever in need of a good laugh I think back to the happenings of one day.

Don Pablo had settled back into his seat—the springs sagging beneath him—after he sold most of the cokes and snacks. A tall husky man came up to his open window, leaned on the door and looked into his eyes—sweat running down his face.

"Hey, I don't have money. Can you give me some water?" he pleaded, removing his hat.

Don Pablo shrugged, his round face still smiling back at him.

"I don't carry water but you can get some from the melted ice in the chest."

The man came around to the back and opened up the chest. There was enough water melted for a drink.

"I need a cup. Give me a cup."

"I don't have cups."

"I have to have a drink right now!" he demanded.

"Well, I do have this can." Don Pablo pulled out the tomato can hanging from the gear shift and handed it out the window. I stared in amazement.

The man scooped up the ice water, leaned back and swigged the water from the can.

"Delicious! That's the best water I ever tasted!" He wiped his forehead on his sleeve as he handed the can over to Don Pablo.

Then I started laughing. I was laughing so hard I had to roll on the ground. Tears were coming out of my eyes.

"What's wrong with him?" The man frowned at me.

"Nothing. You know how kids like to play." He put his finger to his lips to warn me not to say anything.

And I did try but soon I was rolling in the grass, holding onto my stomach because it hurt so much from laughing.

"What's so funny?" He stood over me.

I could hold back no longer. "That's his pee can," I blurted out and continued laughing.

The man turned to see Don Pablo couldn't keep from smiling as well. Then, he started swearing at us and stomped off back to the field. I could see him raising his arms talking to other workers and pointing at the truck. If he wanted sympathy he didn't seem to be getting it. All over the field men were talking and there were waves of laughter rising and falling in the rows.

I decided to be careful, in the future, whenever something is free.

16

Anyone who has older brothers and sisters that tend to get into trouble at school has a lot to overcome. Although he was a great runner for the track team my older brother Marco's reputation did not help mine. On a snowy day with all the students excited and running about, he went outside and made some snowballs. He carried them into the school hallway. The principal stood at the far end, facing the opposite direction. Marco raised his arm and aimed a snowball at him, throwing hard.

It didn't hit the principal but instead hit the light fixture overhead. It shattered and glass flew everywhere. The hall went dark and everyone panicked. Marco disappeared quickly out the side door but a teacher had seen him. My brother got suspended — not for the first time.

Teachers tended to blame me for things I didn't do, though I must say I do like to play jokes.

One day, Jimmy, one of my friends who didn't like school very much, arrived there with a big smile. He unzipped his jacket and showed me that he carried a bottle of something in an inside pocket.

"What have you got there?" I wanted to know. I slowed down to walk beside him.

"Itching powder." He waited for my reaction.

I thought he was probably making it up. "Sure," I told him. "Where did you get it?"

"Oh, we went downtown on the weekend. There was a store that had all kinds of stuff for practical jokes—like rubber throw up."

I watched as he went up to a classmate to pat him on his back and spread a little powder down the back of his neck. That boy was soon itching and scratching like crazy.

"Hey! What's going on?" He took off his sweatshirt and shook it out in the hallway. Soon other students were scratching.

I went into my class and took my seat in the back. Jimmy came in and bent beside Jenny—a very pretty girl who sat in her desk quietly. He looked like he was whispering a secret. Then I saw his hand near her neck.

After he went to his desk she wiggled and squirmed, then she was scratching. She raised her hand. "Teacher, may I go to the restroom?" She dashed out of the room.

In a very short time three other students were scratching and complaining. One boy wiggled so much he knocked over his desk.

"What's going on here? Do we have fleas in the classroom?" The teacher couldn't hold anyone's attention.

"Fleas! Fleas!" More students jumped to their feet and shook out their clothes.

"Teacher, let me go to the nurse. I don't have fleas but I itch all over." A girl pleaded.

With many people wiggling and scratching and the mention of fleas the rest of the class began to feel itchy. The teacher lost control. Some students were crying.

Jimmy managed to spread it far and wide before the teachers caught on. One person after another wiggled and squirmed and shook out their clothes with no relief.

Before noon, four different classes held kids who couldn't sit still in their desks. The more they scratched, the worse they felt. Teachers couldn't teach with so many students scratching...and then itching— more. Some were crying.

Because everyone thought that fleas caused the trouble, they drew back from the scratchers. After a while it was obvious it was something else. When they found out it was itching powder there was a huge uproar. Students from those four classes were sent home to wash it off.

My friend was laughing at everyone and thought it was a great joke. Because I knew who brought the powder, I was able to avoid getting any on myself. This fact and my family name led to suspicion of me as an instigator.

I was brought into the principal's office.

"Simon, did you bring itching powder to school?"

"No, sir, I didn't," I answered, looking the principal in the eyes. But, I couldn't keep my lips from curling upward.

"Are you sure?" he asked again, with a frown. The office was full of parents and the secretary was making phone call after phone call. Anger showed in their faces.

"Well, then do you know who brought it?"

To this question I gave no answer. For sure I knew the culprit but I stuck to a code. I do not tell on my friends or turn them in.

"I will be contacting your parents." He added.

This statement did make me smile. Who were they going to call? Notes home were a waste of time. Occasionally a truant officer would knock on our door, looking for one of my brothers or sisters but it was easy to tell who was there and not open the door.

I was sent into another room and Jimmy was brought into the office.

I heard some crying and then silence. Then, they called me back in. Jimmy was no where to be seen.

"We have been told that you are the one responsible. You are suspended from school for three days. Don't ever do something like that again! You are endangering the whole school! Do you understand?" The principal's stern face held me fast.

I couldn't believe it. Had Jimmy lied and blamed me? I had not told on him. I'm sure my face showed my anger. "That's not true! I had nothing to do with the itching powder," I insisted, raising my voice.

But who did *they* believe? What use is a friend who will even lie about you to save himself? I was sent home with a note. It was hard to explain to my mother why I would be home for three days.

17

Dr. Welch slapped the desk and I looked up, bringing me out of my memories. It was another day and again he grew impatient with me because I never talked. I knew he was getting paid to be there, anyway.

"I know you can speak. Help me out here. I need something to go on. Tell me about your brothers and sisters," he insisted, twisting his head sideways and looking into my eyes as if he could see right into my head. I returned his stare without blinking.

I knew that if I told him what he wanted — none of us would be allowed to remain at home. I would say nothing. I would give him no ammunition to attack.

My brothers and sisters — all eleven of us that still lived. And the sister that had disappeared! Each so different!

My oldest sister, Martha.....she was lovely! She had carried more than her share of responsibilities, as the new brothers and sisters followed, year after year. Until I came along and was born in a hospital, she had come to the conclusion that the doctor who came to our home every year brought the new little one in his black bag. She could cook beans and roll out tortillas at the age of eight. She tried to please our father.

A young man saw her sweetness and took her away from us as his bride when she was seventeen. She was happy to move to a government housing apartment where there was real running water. Everyone missed her. I noticed that my brother-in-law was not as nice to her as he had been before the marriage. She would invite us over, sometimes, when he was not home. They soon made me an uncle.

Then there was Lily. She was a wild river boiling over, at times, but impossible to ignore. She spoke in a very loud voice. Her arms were very strong from field work. She protected the younger ones at school. No one dared to pick on me when she was in the same school as I was.

Too bad she had not been at school that day. I probably wouldn't be in this trouble now.

One day she went to a friend's house instead of coming home after school. I don't know what happened but she didn't come home at all that night and everyone was looking for her. When they did find her and drag her home there was a lot of yelling. She was about fourteen or fifteen and my father was very, very angry.

I just remember him taking out his belt and beating and beating her. There was no place to hide at home. She was crying and screaming at him. He could not tame her on the inside. Then, the next day she ran away—some people said she ran across the river and then to interior Mexico. I don't know how or if she survived. That was years ago. When I think of her, I think of courage. She was unbreakable. Boundaries and borders were not something she understood.

My mother often washed and ironed clothes for the neighbors for a few dollars. She had a big tub of water outside, with a washboard. Some of us helped wring out the larger pieces by grabbing an end and twisting. She really enjoyed heating the iron on the wood stove and pressing the clothes—giving a sharp crease to the pants. She even ironed underwear. She kept hangers on a post that stuck out from the wall. We knew the very nice, new clothes belonged to others.

One evening my brother Marco was getting ready to go to a dance at the parish hall. His hair was very slick and he put on a clean pair of pants. He couldn't seem to find a shirt that was clean. He looked up at the nice clothes along the wall and picked out a lavender and blue pinstriped shirt. It looked like new. He slipped it on and buttoned the front. It fit like it was made for him!

Later, I stopped in at the dance, although I knew I still smelled of onions from the field. Marco was looking great. His long black hair hung loose down his back. Besides bravado, he had rhythm and style and was a very good dancer.

He was holding a pretty girl close when a neighbor boy about the same age approached him.

"Hey, I like your new shirt! "

"Thanks," he nodded, stone-faced.

"Yeah, my mom just bought me one just like that!"

"Is that so?" He steered the girl in a different direction.

The boy followed for a bit, then left. My brother's reputation kept a lot of people from pushing him.

The next morning the shirt was back in place on the hanger, slightly rumpled but ready to go.

Some of the babies that were born after me died as infants. Several brothers carried the same name as those that had died before them.

They brought tiny Lazaro home. He was born early but lived. He was put into a shoebox as a bed — because his body was so very small.

One little sister got pneumonia and died at the age of two. My mother cried over each of them. Dr. Welch did not need to know about them.

18

Faustino

Of my many brothers and sisters the one closest to me in age—just one year older—was Faustino.

My peaceful brother, Faustino...among all of us, was the kindest, the sweetest. I could picture him sitting and smiling at our games. He was born with a weak heart so he wasn't able to run or play with the rest of us. He had a little box of bugs that he collected from the desert—walking sticks, preying mantises, even stinkbugs, sometimes a lizard or a toad. He liked to tend to them and tried to keep them from fighting. They enchanted him. He would put sticks and leaves into the box and watch their tiny faces.

Other memories drifted in like clouds.

One winter it had been very cold and the potbellied stove that heated our tiny home developed a crack and so they removed it to prevent a fire. Its smokestack left a six inch hole in the roof and no one covered it. Many of us huddled together on the two beds, trying to stay warm under the quilts my mother had made.

That night it snowed and we awoke to find the yard white and lovely. Everyone was excited---running about and shouting. Faustino was still sleeping and when we looked over at him, his head held a layer of snow—shining like a crown. We all laughed and Faustino awoke and laughed with us. Nothing ever bothered him. He was serene.

By springtime that year, although he turned eight years old, he wasn't strong enough to go to school anymore. One day my mother took him on the bus to town to shop with her, and he came into the house with a little paper bag full of the Mexican candy that we loved. He was very excited. With a big smile, he gave each one of us a piece and told us he would give us another one the next day.

That night, in a reverse of his usual habit, he wanted the light out and the blankets covering his face. Sometime in the early morning hours the angels came for him and he must have left running, as he never could before. Our mother awoke us all and it was very quiet. His little bag of candy lay beside him, but no one cared about it anymore.

Sorrow splashed over us in unexpected waves that year and many more and the world was meaner. Faustino, my gentle brother, I will never forget you.

19

My father did not like to hear us when he was home. He thought it was rude for children to speak when adults were present, although he spoke rarely. I guess that's why I liked to visit all our neighbors.

We had one very helpful neighbor — one who influenced my father. With his gentle urging we eventually made some progress.

This event changed life at home forever and almost ended mine. Electricity had come to our neighborhood long ago. Everyone around us had lights and power and connected to the outside world with radio and television — but not our family. Even my grandmother had lights in her small tidy home. My father never saw any need.

This neighbor, Eduardo Montes, watched us struggling. He was the same man who helped turn our dirt floor to cement. One day he drew my father aside and talked to him about the benefits of electricity and how it really didn't cost that much. He already had to pay for ice all the time to keep his beer cold in the cooler and there was a way of getting a refrigerator if we had power. Mr. Montes knew a man who could put in the wires for only fifty dollars and we wouldn't have to pay all at once.

Just the possibility of having electricity thrilled us! One day I came home from school and found a tall man wearing gloves and a tool belt stringing wires and putting in receptacles. On the kitchen side he installed an overhead light with a pull switch and one outlet for a plug and on the bed side he attached another pull-switch light and two more outlets fastened into the adobe wall. The wires were strung in plain sight along the walls and ceiling. There was a box that had two fuses.

I was fascinated by all of this—I had reached thirteen and imagined myself a kind of Edison in the way I liked to experiment with whatever I could find. I took apart old lawn mowers and other engines. Electricity now would give me more lighted hours and new possibilities.

In a few more days a small refrigerator plugged into the kitchen outlet appeared. It had a slot to insert quarters. This is the way we could pay for it. So many hours it would run on a quarter and the salesman told us we would own it in a short time. No one did the math to see how much it would actually cost but it was wonderful to get ice cubes and cold water on a hot day! We emptied the ice trays almost as soon as the water was frozen. We even ate the ice that grew inside the refrigerator.

There was a slight problem, however. My brother Marco investigated its mechanism to collect the quarters. Whenever it would run out of time, somehow he would give my mother a shiny quarter and she was happy. He usually had some money for extras.

The man who collected the quarters arrived on a weekend and opened it up to find but two inside. He started yelling at all of us and insisted we pay right away or he would take it away.

My father liked it for his cold beer. Between his present job and making Marco pay up we got to keep the machine.

In the desert hills above our neighborhood ran dirt roads and random piles where people dumped their garbage. I loved to search for treasures. Sometimes I found books that were interesting to read. If I came across old photos of people, I would put them in my pocket and pretend they were my relatives, or if it was a girl — my girl friend. There were also pieces of electric motors and parts.

One day I picked up a small radio that still had a wire and plug and didn't look too bad — just a missing dial — but I could find something to turn it.

I thought it would be nice to have music in our home and carried it back, along with other odd pieces. I tightened some screws and wiped the dirt from it until it shone. I plugged it into the wall and used pliers to turn the dial. Pretty soon mariachi music filled the room. My brothers and sisters were thrilled. My mother rocked to the music and took a few dance steps. She rolled tortillas in time to the music.

There was no way to turn it off so I decided to unplug it. I pulled on the cord and it came away with the radio but left one of the prongs still in the wall. I thought, okay, I will just pull it out with the pliers.

The second I grabbed the prong electricity poured through me. It gave me a tremendous jolt of pain and I couldn't let go. My hand was glued to the pliers and the wall while my body shook uncontrollably. No one had told me of the dangers of electricity! That might have been the end of me!

Thank God, my oldest brother, Ricardo, saw me and knew enough to go to the box and pull the switch! After that, I respected the power of electricity a hundred times more.

Mr. Montes, the neighbor who convinced my father to put in electricity, was also the neighbor who let us watch TV through his window. One summer day I came home to find a TV set on top of a dresser at our own house, and my father sitting on the bed with half a watermelon and a spoon. We hoped he would leave some for us. He was laughing and eating. He loved cartoons! For a while he would come home from work on time to watch the four-o-clock cartoons.

I still liked to search for treasure at the dump. One summer night the rain came down steadily. The next morning I knew the fields would be heavy with mud and there would be no work.

It was a great day to walk the two miles to the dump. I breathed deeply the cool, damp air filled with the incense of wet creosote bushes as I crossed the desert paths. Jackrabbits bounded ahead of me. What would I find today?

When school ended and kids were home, a lot of people cleared away stuff from their houses. As I approached, I saw a big box above a fresh pile of junk. This looked promising. *What could be inside?*

I kicked the side of it to make sure no snakes were hiding. Nothing moved so I unfolded the top of the box. I couldn't believe it! It held glass tubes and bottles and jars filled with hundred of different things — a huge chemistry set! There were instructions and pictures of lots of types of experiments. Who knew what I could do with this?

The box weighed a great deal, but I was determined to carry it all home. If it was left here it would probably be discovered by someone else. I put it on my shoulder and struggled for a ways before I had to set it down and rest my arms. It took me a long time to get home. In the meantime, my imagination raced away.

When I walked in my brothers and sisters were curious. "What's in that huge box?" they asked.

I didn't let them look into it but set it next to the outside wall of the house. I waited until everyone was asleep and then brought the box inside and opened it.

Carefully, I set out the jars and tubes on the table. With the aid of a picture, I saw how to attach one tube to another using corks and pipes. I mixed some chemicals in a jar and watched them change color.

I put together a very large contraption of connected tubes and pipes. It reached so high that I had to stand on a chair. At one end was a bottle of chemicals that I had combined to make a purple-colored mixture. At the other end I put a cork stopper into a glass tube. Now, I stood back to admire it. It looked spectacular!

I swirled the jar and waited. Nothing happened. Then, I saw in the picture that they had a little flame below the jar. *So that's what you do!*

The stove was very close to the table so I slid the apparatus close to the heat. I was very excited. *What had I invented?*

All of a sudden there was a huge noise. **Kaboom!** My experiment exploded and glass went flying everywhere. It hit my face and I started screaming, "My eyes! My eyes!"

My father came running from the other room. He yelled at me. "What have you done, now?"

I continued screaming. My eyes were burning. I was afraid that I was blind.

"Look at that great big spot on the ceiling!" My father yelled.

Everyone in the house was now awake and trying to find out what happened. There was shattered glass stuck to the adobe walls as well as all over the floor. My mother gave me a rag to clean my face and slowly I regained some of my sight.

"Throw all of that away! And I don't want you to ever bring anything from the dump again! You just cause trouble!" My father continued to scold. He didn't seem to care about my eyes.

After that incident many people talked about me like I was crazy. I didn't care what they said. I had many ambitious dreams.

20

Dr. Welch's frustration was mounting. He resorted to more threats.

"If you won't talk to me, I have no other choice but to sign this paper and send you to reform school!"

Wham!" He slammed a clipboard onto his desk.

I thought about it seriously. *Did he have that authority?* It was a possibility. What was reform school like? My older brothers went in and out of it like it had swinging doors. But I never wanted that kind of life. I decided if I really didn't want to experience it, I was going to have to talk a little—but I knew better than to say very much. I knew how to circle the conversation and protect the rest of us at home.

"I didn't do anything wrong."

"Why did you hit him?" he asked directly.

"If somebody hits you, don't you have the right to hit back?" I redirected, boldly returning his stare.

"Are you saying that he started the fight?" Dr. Welch rose to his feet and walked closer.

"Have you seen how big Ron is—a head taller and more than twice my weight?" I threw back at him.

"No, but I read a report from about his injuries. They were serious! He suffered a great deal."

"And you think that I am responsible?" I glared at him.

"It is hard to believe that you could hurt a classmate like that."

I could see he was sizing up my small frame. He didn't know anger and years of work formed steel within me. I would not tell the real events of that day. Maybe he was forming doubts in his head. I could spin tales that he would follow that ended nowhere. I was going to feed him bits and pieces and let him think he came by himself to the conclusion that I wanted. I could play his game and make it mine.

For some time we had not seen my father. This was not unusual except it had been so long the big flour sack was now empty and there were no more beans. We scrounged for food — showing up at friends' houses just at mealtime, leaning in the doorway until someone invited us in or gave us a plate.

"Dad's working out of town. He's got a job with a railroad," my mother lied.

"When is he coming back?" We wanted to know.

There was no grocery store nearby. My mother would earn a few dollars washing clothes. She had an old Maytag winger washing machine now. She carefully pressed out the wrinkles and made creases with an iron that she heated on the wood stove.

My father had the only car. We were all aware that something needed to happen and soon. My mother knew how to keep secrets. I tried to help out by working odd jobs after school.

At the junior high it was hard to concentrate. Life outside of school seemed so much more pressing. I wore raggedy clothes and ill-fitting shoes and was always hungry, except for the lunch I ate after helping the kitchen crew. What I did sport was toughness and a reputation. I was small for my age but all that work had given me strong arm muscles and I did not hold back.

I joked with my friends but with others I was very irritable and quick to take offense. Bigger boys would try to look mean and shove others around – but I never stood for it. I was known for an instant response to anything at all and few tried to bother me. I smoked cigarettes when I could get them, though not at school. I knew how to distract a teacher and disrupt a class but mostly I still liked to learn about the world away from home.

The second weekend in May stretched out gray and ugly even though the sun shone. I rose early and hoed in the fields near the river. When I went for my pay the foreman looked at me and said, "Come next week. I can't pay you today." I wiped my forehead and pleaded with my eyes.

My younger brothers and sister whined, "I'm hungry. When is Dad coming home?" I looked at my mother whose mouth turned down and had little to say – unlike her usual self. Tomorrow was Mexican Mothers' Day and there was little we could do. She was boiling water on the stove to wash clothes for the neighbor's family.

"Help me put this in the washer."

The wringer washing machine stood in the front yard. It helped to water the one hardy elm tree that survived our neglect and shaded us in the summer. I swung the boiling hot pot off the wood stove and pushed open the screen door that was so broken the flies felt very welcome inside. I wanted to help in whatever way I could. Even though my father was not very fatherly, at least, before, he had been there. Now, we yelled at each other and fought. I was afraid my mother was going to give up and leave all of us. She really deserved a better life.

That Sunday I rose early to chop wood for the stove. I hoped there was something to eat. The morning was cool and a soft wind blew through the cottonwoods across the street.

A car horn honked and my father's car rolled into the yard. The rest of the family scrambled outside. The younger ones yelled, "Papá!"

He opened his door and got out. *But wait! What was going on?* There was someone else in the front seat. It was a woman with scarlet lips, blue-shadowed eyes, big earrings jangling, and she was smiling triumphantly at all of us. I looked at my mother. Her eyebrows were raised and she looked like she was about to say something, then turned away.

"Do you want groceries?" My father asked.

What a stupid question! He knew we were starving.

My mother looked around at her brood of children standing about. We were all she had left. The older ones had left as soon as they could. Then she put on a mysterious smile and went to get her shoes. I watched her in her humiliation get in the back seat and accept a ride and I knew she did it for all of us. But I hated him then. I hated him with a black hatred that grew within me and threatened to grow and explode. The others were too young to understand.

"Good. We are going to eat," they cried.

The next week at school I had a hard time paying attention. Visions of our family crumbling apart as the "other woman" smiled from my father's car interrupted my thoughts. And then along came Ron...a big boy—at least fifty pounds heavier than me, a football player. He pushed me in the hallway between classes and for some reason I let it go. I went on to my class. He turned to his friends and winked.

At lunchtime my friends told me that they heard him bragging to his friends.

"I beat up Simon Palomar on the weekend." They looked at him with unbelief. No one before had beat me. I knew how to fight and had a scary reputation. My classmates had not challenged me. Soon it was all over the school.

I could not let this go. I had nothing left but my reputation and what he said was a total lie.

"He said that?" I asked a friend.

"Yes. Everybody heard him and he went into detail how he made you cry."

"Where is he?" If I let this go I was finished and anyone could walk all over me.

"Coming out of the lunchroom."

I handed my schoolwork to my friend Pete and went into the hallway. It was not hard to find Ron. He was a head taller than I was and stood with his back to me and I heard him relating to his friends the gory details of how he had beat me up.

"So, you beat me up, did you? Do you want to try it again?"

His big dirty blonde head swung around and I saw his eyes narrow in fear. He raised his hands as he tried to back away but his friends crowded in behind.

I swung at his face and hit him on the chin. His head rocked back and I pummeled him in the stomach. He flailed at me but I had the anger of ten and battered at his face.

"*Fight! Fight!*" rang out in the hallway as I knocked him backwards and he fell on the stairway. I couldn't stop myself. I went after him as if he was the cause of all my disappointments. I picked him up and banged his head against the metal locker. He was bleeding and people were screaming as I punched him…. Then… my mind went blank.

21

The next time I was brought to see Dr. Welch he was accompanied by several other men in white and blue jackets. Two were fumbling with some machinery that had wires attached.

"Simon, I think we can help you with your anger problem."

I raised my left eyebrow as a question.

"We have a treatment that should help you to feel better and to relax. We think your brain has not been responding correctly." Dr. Welch tapped the top of his head as if I couldn't understand his words well enough.

They brought me to a padded chair and had me sit in it. It had nice arm rests and I felt upheld by the chair as I leaned back in it.

"Take this pill. It will calm you." I was handed a red pill and a small paper cup of water. They watched carefully. I had to swallow it—not like some other times that I had let pills drop into a sleeve and then disposed of them later.

A thin gray-haired man pointed to the machine that they had brought into the room. "We are going to attach some electrodes to your head and apply a very low voltage of electricity. Research has shown how it can restructure brain waves and correct improper behavior patterns. You don't have to do anything or say anything. It shouldn't hurt. It will just feel like twinkling lights. Think of it as a massage for you head." He smiled reassuringly.

All over my head they taped wires. I couldn't see how many or exactly where. *Were they really about to give me a bad shock?* Finally they strapped my arms to the chair. I remembered the broken prong on the radio cord.

"This is just for you protection so you don't pull something out and hurt yourself," the gray-haired man told me in a way that sounded kind.

What was I going to do? At least I didn't have to talk. I squeezed my eyes tightly closed and waited.

Soon the machine was whirring and lights were blinking above me. Powerful pulses made my head throb. *Were they experimenting on me?* I'm sure they knew no one would complain about my treatment. The shocks were not strong enough to be painful but thinking became difficult.

After a while, Dr. Welch loosened and removed the straps on my arms. I opened my eyes to his stare.

"We are removing the electrodes, now. It might pull a little on your hair," he apologized.

I found it hard to focus on anything in the room. I was afraid that if I stood I might fall.

"In a few days they are going to let you go, but every week you must agree to come here to see me." I stared blankly at Dr. Welch's all too familiar cold face.

"You will be allowed to go back to school the rest of the year and start again in the fall. You will leave from school and come here to talk to me. I am issuing you a pass for the bus. You will need to transfer from San Jacinto Plaza downtown. Do you know where that is?"

I nodded slowly.

"There are going to be restrictions on your activities. I will tell you more about that later."

I let my mouth curl slightly at the edges. I did not want him to see my excitement.

It was not long before the door swung open and I walked out to take in the smell of city air. I caught the bus home, smiling at everyone I faced.

22
Beverley

That summer did provide some amusements. When I wasn't working, I hung out with guys who also saw troubles at home and tried to make sense of life.

We would gather to talk and joke and make fun of each other. We weren't very well informed by parents about some subjects and so tried to find out for ourselves. One friend, who was older and had some respect from us, because he wasn't afraid to fight anyone, gathered us to tell us about girls. According to his account a girl could get pregnant by kissing a boy. For a while we took this very seriously.

One day Roger came by to get me. He was my age and lived a few houses down the street. He hurriedly took me up to the hills where he had hidden something in the arroyo and he wouldn't tell me what it was. At first all I saw was red lips, long blonde hair and a fancy dress. *Who was it?*

When I got closer I realized she wasn't moving and she was made of plastic. A store that had closed down had left *Beverley* leaning against the dumpster and Roger had rescued her. She was very tall and beautiful. What a find!

We started to make plans for her. Upon examination we found that she separated at the waist by unscrewing her top and bottom. If we didn't want anyone to see us carrying her about we could each take a half and put her back together later. Her face and long blonde hair were very lifelike.

Beverley became popular among our friends and developed a life all her own. She started to hide out in boys' bedrooms and wear their sister's clothes. She was kept secret and wrapped tight in blankets as she was transported. People would get glimpses of her everywhere. If we went to the ditch to swim, she liked to be placed standing alongside, with a long arm in the air. She hung out with us in make-shift clubhouses. If we saw someone coming close, we wrapped her up and moved her quickly. When she was in two pieces she was easy to sling under an arm or over a shoulder by two boys.

It didn't take long for the women in the neighborhood to become suspicious. They weren't sure what they saw. We stuck together and never let her stay in one place for any length of time; but, it was impossible to keep her totally hidden because she was so popular. Then, our mothers grilled us.

"Who was that blonde girl hanging around?" Roger's mother asked.

"Nobody, Mom."

"I saw someone leaving last night. Whose friend is she?" She put her hands on her hips and demanded an answer.

"I don't know anybody like that," he answered innocently.

"Well, you better watch out!"

"Mom, my dress is missing and I think I saw Roger in the desert with a blonde girl that was wearing one just like it," added his sister, indignantly.

"Roger, if there is anything funny going on, you are going to have to answer for it!" His mother threatened.

My mother didn't hold back either. "We've seen that white girl that is hanging around here. You all had better leave her alone! If she turns up pregnant they're going to check it out and find out who the father is." She scowled at me with her hands on her hips.

I had to run a distance away into the arroyo because I had to laugh and to hold back was so hard. I repeated her comments to my friends and we roared with laughter at the thought of a pregnant *Beverley*. They were all getting the same lectures at home.

Beverley had many adventures. It was Roger who came up with one of the best. Mr. Mendez lived down the street and everyone knew he liked to drink a little, actually, quite a lot. Sometimes he worked nights and slept in the daytime while his wife worked.

An afternoon when we saw Mr. Mendez walking with wobbly legs into his home, Roger got the idea of slipping *Beverley* next to him in bed. We dressed her in night clothes and sent a lookout to make sure no one was watching. Roger peeked in the window to see Mr. Mendez passed out and snoring on his bed. The door was always unlocked so it was easy to bring her inside and lay her beneath the blankets with her head resting on the pillow next to him. We smoothed down her hair and raised one of her arms above her head. He didn't stir.

Then we were on the lookout for Mrs. Mendez. She usually had no patience for us or other kids in the neighborhood. As she approached on the street Roger ran up to her. He couldn't wait to spit it out.

"Mrs. Mendez, Mrs. Mendez." He practically jumped up and down.

"What do you want now?" She snarled.

"I just have to warn you."

"What's going on?" She slowed her stride to face him.

"Mr. Mendez has someone at the house. I think a blonde lady."

"He does, does he? We'll see about that." She scowled and swung her purse beside her. We ran alongside as she came to the house.

We heard her scream as she came into the bedroom. "Get out! Get out! You, hussie!" And then she was banging her husband with her purse and dragging him out of the bed. He was moaning and groaning loudly as he tried to wake up.

We looked at each other. It was time to rescue *Beverley*. Mr. Mendez remained in a kind of stupor as we entered the bedroom. His wife's angry yelling had disoriented him. We saw him look over at *Beverley's* head on the pillow and open his eyes wide in astonishment. Taking advantage of the huge hullabaloo, we quickly wrapped her in a sheet and cradled her between us and hustled out the door. Outside, we ran to the arroyo, laughing and struggling for breath in our hurry to get away without being caught.

Word of that blonde woman rose and fell all over the neighborhood. One person claimed they had seen Mr. Mendez drinking with that woman. Everyone was on the lookout for that tall shameless blonde!

Not long after that we decided *Beverley* was starting to look a little raggedy and scratched. With everyone on the look out for her it was more and more difficult for her to remain hidden.

She was going to have to meet her end. She was just too valuable to be thrown into a dumpster. We needed something more fitting and exciting. Again it was Roger who came up with the best plan.

"I think she needs to jump off something."

"How about from a cliff up in the mountains?" I suggested.

"No, she likes drama. How about the overpass on the freeway that they just built? She would get everybody's attention!"

"Wow! I will be sad to see her go, but no one will recognize her if she gets run over. They will always remember her as a real girl around here." We laughed and told our friends to gather tomorrow evening for the big event.

We held a small going away party for her. We knew we would be sad at her departure. She was our best girlfriend. She never asked for anything and never complained. She was always willing to listen.

We brushed her hair and dressed her in a fancy red dress thanks to one boy who had a sister with a nice wardrobe. We cleaned her face. She was starting to be a little loose at her center joint because she had to be hidden in two parts so many times. She wore high heels and somebody added a blue beaded necklace.

We drank sodas and ate chips and told stories about *Beverley* and her famous adventures as we waited for darkness to fall. It was kind of like a wake before her death.

To the west a beautiful red and orange sunset glowed as we picked her up, wrapped in a blanket and walked to the overpass. We leaned over. Below, cars and trucks flew by in all four lanes. Some of us shook her hand, others gave her a big hug as she shed the blanket and stood by the railing.

We waited for a big truck. Then, we dropped her feet first and watched as she bounced a little below. The vehicles screeched as they applied brakes and swerved to the side. We heard a crack as the wheels of a large truck couldn't change paths and rolled over her body. Cars stopped and people popped out and ran back to help.

It was time for us to leave. We headed back away from the freeway, as inconspicuously as possible, separating quickly.

Later that night we heard there had been a bad accident on the freeway. A woman had jumped and had died when she was run over—a blonde.

After that, she became a legend. No one but the group of us knew her well and we never told others. We just laughed when we thought of the good times we had with her.

I don't know how many marriages she nearly broke up, or how many boys were warned about getting her pregnant.

23

In the fall, when I returned to school, I had a new reputation—as "el loco", and I intended to use it. Yes, I was crazy—crazy like a fox. Every week at 11:00 on Thursday I was released from school and I took the bus to the downtown plaza where all the city buses came, and made my transfer to the hospital. When I got there, I came in a side door to a scrubbed-clean office and signed in at the desk. I waited until I was called in.

Dr. Welch continued to question me. I almost never gave him any answers. Sometimes I would amuse myself my making some comment that caused him to scribble furiously in a notebook, and get all excited. When he found he had followed a false path he would look dejected. He was getting more and more frustrated and knew he was wasting his time. But I was sure he was getting paid very, very well. At last he threw his hands in the air.

"I can't help you! Promise you won't cause trouble and you won't need to come here anymore."

I nodded my head slowly and thoughtfully. My family was not investigated. I had not told.

At home, nothing was getting easier. My father drove to the neighborhood every week to visit his mother who lived up the street. Only occasionally would he come by our house. If he gave my siblings a quarter, they were happy with him. Once in a while he gave my mother a little money for groceries. She was over forty-five years old and pregnant with my youngest sister. She did whatever she could to earn a little money—washing and ironing clothes for the neighbors. She cooked beans and made stacks of tortillas for other families.

When I wasn't in school I worked as much as possible. I took down trees, pulled out stumps, worked with landscapers and mowed lawns as well as field work.

My oldest brother had a job with a landscaping crew and worked steadily. The only trouble was he used the money to drink and have fun with his friends and tried to borrow back from my mother what he had given her earlier in the week.

My brother Marco had left school a long time ago but hadn't settled down to really work anywhere. He had a lot of other interests. He was expert at telling stories. He wasn't too interested in sticking with the truth when he could spin a colorful tale that entertained his friends.

My mother sent him to Los Angeles to stay with her sister, hoping he would work and send money home. His temper kept him from holding a job for very long, but he did like California.

After a long absence he showed up back home with his black hair loose and flowing to his waist. He wore boots, jeans and a black t-shirt with the sleeves cut off showing his large biceps that were now covered with tattoos. One arm had the face of an Indian chief and some arrows. The other arm displayed a large cross and other symbols.

A trailer park rented spaces nearby and there were a lot of Anglo families that lived there. Many of them worked at the racetrack and did not always stay year-round. Some boys living there were close to Marco's age and knew him well. They admired his tough reputation and loved to listen to him.

When they saw him outside standing in the shade of the rock wall that surrounded the park they came right over.

"Marco! You're back! How was California?" I could see Johnny, Timmy and Don were excited.

"I had a good time."

My brother waited until they were close to him, leaned back and lit a cigarette. He blew some smoke and continued. "You know the president of the Hell's Angels died when I was there."

"Really?" They were eager for more.

"And they elected me to drive lead motorcycle." He paused.

"Wow! That's crazy!"

Now he had their rapt attention and he continued, painting the picture, making them feel like they were there.

"Yes, I drove the lead bike of a hundred-and-fifty motorcycle funeral procession. Just imagine it! We had a police escort in front. I rode a big black chopper smoking a joint." (He inhaled, then made the rough noise of a motorcycle — Vroooom!.)

"I had a big blonde Mama riding behind, hugging me, her hair flying back. People pointed to me as we rode by. 'Kids, that's Apache Marco driving lead,' they said."

"Amazing!" Their jaws dropped.

"You're kidding! Didn't the police go after you for the pot?" Johnny asked his voice rising with surprise.

"No, they didn't want trouble from anybody so they left us alone. I must have smoked at least five joints in that procession. What were the police going to do? After all, we were at least a hundred-and-fifty motorcycles riding together."

I could see the boys took it all in. They couldn't wait to spread the word among their friends. They knew "Apache Marco"!

That *was* a lot of smoke!

24

My father had left a broken down car parked in our yard…a cherry-red 1955 Chevy. He saw how I was working and told me that if I saved enough money to fix it, it would be mine. He had never given me anything before, so I was filled with new hope for the future. I worked and worked.

After I turned fifteen and my youngest sister was but a few months old I came home to find my father removing all of his belongings from the house, stuffing them in his car. My mother was sitting at the table, wiping her face with her apron. My baby sister was crying and crying and no one paid any attention to her wails.

That was the end! Eighteen children and twenty five years of marriage! Evidently, his new woman didn't want him to stop by anymore.

Later that day two of his friends drove up in a truck and tied a tow rope around the Chevy that I had been promised.

"No! I have the money to fix it now. He promised me this car!" I pleaded.

"That's too bad, Simon. He's having it fixed for the other woman's son. He paid us to take it."

I watched as they pulled it out of the yard, into the street. Soon, the only thing left was the dust.

That was the final straw! He didn't even have the nerve to tell me in person. I shook my head in disbelief. I vowed to keep my word if I promised anybody something. I hated him all the more.

Alcohol was part of life and was freely offered to kids who were old enough to work. I enjoyed the taste of it and the confidence and energy it gave me. It deadened the sadness around me. I found I could drink and drink and it didn't make me sick. On New Year's Eve I could visit most houses up and down the street and have a shot of tequila. If you had money they didn't check for an ID at the stores.

I had the sympathy of many who saw I tried to help my mother. I bought an old truck and used it to do odd jobs and take my mother to the store. She depended on me more and more.

They opened up a new high school that started at my grade. It was located in an area that had many very nice brick houses. Word got around that "Mexicans" weren't wanted at this school. So, of course that ensured that all of us wanted to go to school there. Even though I was in school, my mind was elsewhere, planning ways to make a living.

I discovered that if one is not squeamish, there are a lot of different jobs to make money and to learn at the same time. I dug out and unclogged septic and sewer drain pipes. Some had tree roots that entered the drain. Others were stopped up due to grease and garbage. I knew how to use a plumber's snake. The smell was terrible but the pay was good.

I regularly did yard work for a lady who worked as a nurse. In her area of the city they began replacing the galvanized metal water pipes that went into the houses with copper lines—this was to reduce the amount of lead in the water. I saw how close to the surface the pipes were and how they were arranged. When the new pipes were installed, they left the old pipes on the grass. This gave me an idea.

"Miss Turner, what are you going to do with those pipes?" I asked her.

"Those are of no use to me anymore. I see you have a truck. Could you haul them away for me?" She stood in the doorway of her house with her little, black terrier beside her.

"Sure. I'll be glad to," I let her know. I placed the pipes in the back of the truck as she went inside.

Later, I drove along the street to an area where the city was putting in water lines. Two men were leaning on their shovels under a tree. They looked up as I got out of the truck. "Could you tell me what you have to do to put in a water line?"

They looked at each other, then, the younger one answered. "We put in the meter if you have the pipe laid. Your responsibility is from the meter on to your house. There is a fee to put in the meter."

"How much is the fee?" I wanted to know.

"Right now, it's twenty dollars." He took off his cap. "You have to go pay at the downtown office." He wiped the sweat from his forehead. "If we dig the line for you, it costs more—depends on how far."

"Thanks!" Now I was excited. Lately the water situation had gotten worse at our house. The next door neighbors had refused to let us have water from their hose more than once that week.

My mother and I decided the best place for a faucet would be outside, close to the elm tree. There was no sewer or septic system so for now, this was the best place. I dug a trench and laid the pipe into it. I had learned how to connect elbows and shut-off valves. When I next earned twenty dollars I went downtown and paid for the meter.

When the line was installed, we all gathered around and let the water gush out.

The crazy thing was it was not that hard. I wondered why my father had not put this in years ago.

"Mom, someday you will have a house with inside plumbing," I promised her.

For a while I worked for a rancher who called himself "The Boll Weevil".   When he was drunk he approached people and asked them, "Do you know who I am?"

If they didn't answer quickly enough he would glare at them, raise his arms above his head and shout, "The *Boll Weevil*". When we were delivering hay at the racetrack, his loud drunken voice would make the horses rear.

"Get him out of here!" the trainers yelled. He was a gigantic man and did not hurry.

He asked me to do many different jobs. I cut down trees. I dug out stumps. Sometimes I stacked and loaded hay.

Other times he wanted me to break horses. I didn't have much experience but was willing to try. These were not fancy horses. The idea was just to stay on them until they didn't buck anymore. I landed in the dirt over and over until I was very, very sore and bruised... but, I did break the horses and none of my bones. Mr. Boll Weevil sat on the fence and watched. He paid me five dollars a horse.

Once in a while he told me and others to come back at night. Then, we rode in a truck down by the railroad tracks. Alongside were stacks of old tarred beams that had been used as railroad ties.

"Load up the truck, boys. I have a contract with the railroad."

It was dark and hard to see because he turned off the truck lights. He stood alongside us, smoking, and looked down the tracks. When we had loaded the truck we got back inside and he drove awhile with no headlights. Back on the ranch, after we stacked the ties behind a barn, he pulled out his icebox and gave us beer.

We never asked why it happened to be that we always went at night.

25

Wisconsin (1966)

Early in the summer in which I had turned
sixteen, I came home to find my mother waiting for me,
holding a satchel with a change of clothes inside.

"Son, tomorrow morning you have to be
downtown at seven o'clock."

"Why, Mom? What's going on?" I had no idea
what she wanted.

"You have to be on a bus that is leaving from
Seventh Street—right next to the border bridge. You're
going to another state with other men and work for
three months," she added very seriously.

"No, Mom. Why me? Why do I have to go?" I
demanded.

Then she gave me a fiercely sad look that let me
know for some reason I was the one that needed to help
the others. She couldn't do it all herself.

"Son, there is work for you and you have to send
money home."

I wanted to kick and scream and run away. But I
listened as she clasped her hands together.

"And tell them that you are seventeen. They
won't take anybody sixteen," she added.

I couldn't sleep that night. I went to visit friends. Somebody had a bottle of tequila and we built a fire and stayed out in the desert, talking. I kept trying to think of schemes to get out of this trip. It was no use.

In the early twilight I drove my old truck over to Don Pablo's house and parked it next to the saggy carcass of his old truck in which we had enjoyed so many fun times. I walked inside and joined him and his wife sitting at the table drinking coffee.

I got straight to the point. "Don Pablo, do you want to buy my truck?"

"Why? Don't you need it, my friend?" He set his cup down on the table and turned to me.

"Not now. I have to go on a trip."

"Really? I sure need a truck, but I don't have money now."

"For you I'm selling it for one hundred dollars — and you don't have to pay right away. Just go with me downtown and you can drive it back as yours."

"What a deal! I'll have the money for you when you get back. Let me get dressed."

"I'll be right back for you," I replied, thinking of all the times Don Pablo had been a steady friend. Then, I went home and picked up the clothes my mother had ready, along with a burrito. Hugging and kissing was not something we did.

"Adios. May God bless you on your journey." She stood at the door, rubbing her hands together. "And don't forget to send money," she finished.

I stopped for Don Pablo to make his way out of the house and settle into the truck, then, I headed to town.

At the corner of Seventh Street and Santa Fe—the street that leads to the pedestrian bridge crossing to Juarez I could see a green and yellow bus parked and a line of men standing nearby. Some held in their hands plastic bags or small packs; most wore baseball caps or western hats.

I pulled into an empty parking spot and got out and stood on the sidewalk, while Don Pedro made his way slowly from the passenger seat.

"I've got to thank you, Simon. I can sure use this truck. " He grabbed me and hugged me.

"Don't mention it," I replied and hurried over to the bus. I was afraid that hug was going to make me cry.

Don Pablo adjusted the bench seat of the truck so that he could fit and got into the driver's seat. I took my sack and walked to the end of the line. It was easy to tell that most of the men were native Mexican and did not speak much English. I was sure I was the youngest. Near the open door of the bus was a tall man with a thick black mustache and a clipboard. He was checking off names as the men entered the bus.

"Simon Palomar," the man called as I made my way to the door of the bus.

"That's me," I answered in English.

Surprised that I did not speak in Spanish, he examined my face. "How old are you?"

"Seventeen." I remembered to say.

"Okay. Your mother is Angela Palomar?" I nodded. "I will get the hundred dollars to her." He marked my name off on the list. "Get in." He stayed close to the door as if making sure no one got back out.

I found a seat on the aisle and put my sack beneath the seat. Although the windows were opened all the way, the bus was already stifling hot. It was packed full. I wondered where we were headed but did not want to look ignorant to these men.

The man in the window seat next to me wanted to talk. "Wait until we get up north, it will be cool enough," he commented, as he made sure the window was as wide open as possible.

"How long do you think it takes to get there?" I wondered.

"Wisconsin? Probably two days. Are you ready?"

That gave me a good clue to our destination. I'd heard that factories and farms in the northern states often needed summer workers. They didn't pay attention to where the workers came from or their papers.

The bus held at least forty men. Some of them looked anxious, others sang sad songs of leaving home as the bus pulled out of town onto the new freeway. Others were excited. Although I was nervous about going, at the same time, I always liked a challenge and new experiences and situations.

The bus stopped every couple of hours for gas and for us to stretch our legs and to smoke. There were usually small stores that were open for us to buy snacks and use the bathrooms. Alcohol was not allowed on the bus. I could see and smell a few of the men that had hidden bottles in their bags. People that bought snacks ate them quickly before entering because once they got back inside there were others that claimed they had no money and were hungry.

The town that I remember most was Tulsa, Oklahoma. Here, the bus driver pulled up to a diner. We all go out. It had already been a long ride and we hungered for something other than chips and peanuts. As we started to enter a man with a black apron rushed to the door. He and the driver were yelling at each other. We discovered the restaurant did not want Mexicans inside. After more discussion it was agreed that we could order food — but we had to eat it behind the building. I watched the other men. They were resigned, not surprised. To me, it was a little shocking. This was a raunchy, greasy-looking business. It didn't look like wealthy people ran it — but they were prejudiced. I could see no reason for them to reject our business. I spit on the ground as we got back on the bus.

None of us knew anyone when we began our trip. Although we spent much of the time sleeping, by the time we reached Wisconsin, everyone knew each other.

When we arrived at the small town of Bottoms, the bus pulled into a gravel roadway and screeched to a stop. The air was warm and sticky humid. A foreman wearing a yellow jumpsuit was there to meet us and point us to our dormitory. He knew very little Spanish and I was the only one fluent in English so I had to do some translating. He wanted us to know that we would be working twelve hour days and meals would be provided in a cafeteria and that for this, twenty-five dollars a week would be deducted from our weekly check. Alcohol was not permitted in the camp. This was a canning factory and the vegetables were ripening and we needed to stay working. As he spoke, more buses arrived.

Inside the metal building were rows and rows of beds — over a hundred in all. One end of it held showers, sinks and toilets. At the other end were tables and two refrigerators. Most of us found beds near those we knew from our bus.

The next day a whistle woke us and after breakfast we filed into the factory and were split up into different processing lines. I watched as a machine chopped both ends of ears of corn and then husked them. The yellow kernels flowed onto a conveyor belt. Then, they poured down a chute into the cans. I could see them filling the cans above me through a glass window. They were supposed to make a steady stream.

Another machine placed lids on the cans and sealed them. A man showed me how to make sure the lids and cans were coming together smoothly and sealing completely. There was a switch to stop the machine if there was a problem. Then they were moved into a pressure cooker. Cans that were not well filled or did not seal well floated to the top when they were tested. We snared them and hoisted them out with a large metal basket at the end of a rope and pulley.

I was just getting the hang of working my section of the machine when I looked into the glass window to see the corn kernels coming down the chute accompanied by little white wiggling worms. I immediately threw the switch to turn off the motor. A manager came running over to see what had happened. I pointed out the worms coming with the corn.

The man looked at me and laughed. "Oh, that's all right. They just add a little flavor and some extra protein. They don't hurt anything." He restarted the machine, waved to another man and motioned me back to work.

By the label applied to the cooked cans I realized that this brand of vegetable is sold in many stores. Now I wasn't sure what to think. Canned corn certainly lost some of its appeal for the future.

Everyone settled into their jobs. Loud machines clanked and whirled and pounded. It was very loud. Twelve hours doing the same thing is very boring but the money was okay. Through the next days I learned how to operate more machinery. It was nice to have cafeteria style meals even at lunch and I ate all that I could.

The first weeks went smoothly. Later on, as we started to get our checks we found little to do on our day off and wandered into the town to explore. Many workers were accustomed to drinking in the evening so they had to go into town. As I walked along the sidewalks some people would smile, others would look away or stare at me suspiciously. I tried to be friendly with all those that I met. I found the post office and mailed money orders home and helped others do so.

Before long there was trouble at the bars. So many people couldn't explain what they wanted or needed in English and very few town people knew any Spanish at all. Among the blonde and blue-eyed we stood out like plums on a pear tree.

I soon found myself in the middle of it all. One night Raul Benitez and some of his friends woke everyone up when they came in. Raul's face was smashed up badly. He had a bloody shirt wrapped around his head. His friends were yelling.

"What happened?" We wanted to know.

"There was a fight at Swenson's bar."

"*Porqué?*"

"I don't know what started it. I don't understand it at all. We were just sitting at a table and three men came over and said something to us. Then, one of them started swinging at Raul. We fought back and now Raul's nose is broken!" replied Javier, Raul's friend.

About twenty of the guys dressed hurriedly and followed Javier out the door, headed to town. "If we find anybody we're going to jump on them," they cried.

Everyone knew there was going to be trouble. I tried to go back to sleep even though there was a lot of commotion around me. I *did* like having my own bed.

Sometime after midnight the supervisors and the owner of the camp came into the dining room with some of the men. I could hear a lot of angry shouting in two languages. Then I heard someone saying, "Get Simon. He knows both languages. Where is he?"

They got me out of bed and brought me in the room and I tried to make sense of all the yelling.

"What's going on? Hey, if you want me to get it straight you're going to have to talk one at a time," I told them. I was the youngest there, but I enjoyed the power pushed on me.

"Those town people, they don't like Mexicans! We want to drink and they won't let us. It's not fair! We don't want our people being beat up." My co-workers were all riled up and I translated for them.

"The bar owners called us to pick up the men. There are all kinds of fights going on all over town. You are causing trouble everywhere," the supervisors yelled back at all of us.

"You mean we are good enough to work here, but not to mingle with the people of Bottoms?" I threw back at the supervisors, while trying to sort it all out. Outside I could see a white police car with revolving blue and red lights.

The camp owner glared at me. "We can't have trouble with the police!"

"Then why don't you just let us drink here in the camp?" I suggested. Behind me I could hear a shout of agreement. I guessed they could understand that much English.

"No, that's impossible. It can't be allowed. It's against all the rules." The owner shook his head and looked to his supervisors for approval. The one closest to me shook his head.

I had heard how the other workers felt. "Why not? They feel lonely here, away from their families. They have nothing to do but work. They can police themselves and prevent trouble." The workers behind me nodded at my words.

"Absolutely no alcohol!" The owner stood his ground.

"Okay, don't expect anybody to show up for work tomorrow," I threw back. "We were guaranteed three months work or else you have to pay for tickets for all of us to return home. That was in the contract." I had heard all about this on the trip up here.

At this point one supervisor brought the sheriff over and pointed to me. "Throw him in jail. He's the instigator!"

"Wait a minute. You pulled me out of bed to translate. I didn't cause all of this," I replied, glancing around at all the men.

"What's going on?" They wanted to know. Their faces showed worry.

"They want to put me in jail," I informed them in Spanish.

"No! You are the youngest here. They can't do that! If they take you, they have to take all of us." They came up and surrounded me.

I was very happy to translate this. Then the second supervisor took the owner aside and told him, "If there is no alcohol, there will be no work and the camp will be empty. It's too late to get more workers."

The owner sighed loudly, and said, "Okay, then, I don't like it but let them have their alcohol."

The crowd around me let out a big cheer.

Then the sheriff and owner came over and shook my hand and told me, "The rules are—you can drink but there can be no fights and no damage. No trouble. Agreed?"

I explained the rules to the men and they shook hands with the owner. We agreed to police ourselves— to deal with anybody that started to get rowdy.

The mood inside the camp improved after that day. Alcohol was brought in from the outside but no one drank in the town. I was happy that I could drink, too. I already had a taste for alcohol. If there was any friction in the camp a group of the more stable men dealt with the problem. No one wanted to lose the privilege of alcohol in the camp.

The supervisors were happy. The owner was happy — especially when the three months were up and it was time for us to go. He made sure I was on the first bus to leave.

"Are you going to want me back next year?" I questioned him as I got on.

"No!" was the brief answer.

What had started as a feeling of being sold down the river turned into a trip that widened my horizons in every way. That was not my only contract job. I went to other cities and towns and learned a lot of different skills. I worked in factories and on tree farms. I worked on construction sites and learned carpentry. I continued to enjoy drinking.

It was in a bar I made a connection with a foreman and went to work for the Sioux railroad. I had a place in town but we traveled for weeks, doing section work — repairing and replacing tracks and railroad ties. We lived in a train car as we moved along. I saw a lot of beautiful country and experienced some really cold weather.

When I returned from my working trips, nothing ever seemed to change at home.

None of the older ones had much ambition. My sisters had babies, my brothers drank. My younger brother Nate spent a lot of time with friends and their families who trained and rode horses. He didn't like school much and was waiting until he was fifteen and could leave school and become an apprentice jockey. I didn't seem to have a whole lot in common with anybody, except I loved to drink—like a lot of my friends.

Inside all of us was a longing for a real family that cared and stuck together. No matter how hard I tried it just didn't happen. I started to think about having a family of my own, someday. I resolved to be totally different from my father.

26

Zelene

Zelene chose to attend college far away from her home in the Northwest. She had never traveled to El Paso before. She had gone to see the University of Texas Miners play the Seattle U team and lose — their only loss of that famous season in which they won the national title. Orange was her favorite color and watching the flashy antics of the team playing in the bright orange confirmed her choice of colleges.

The thought of living along a major river, and a city that bordered Mexico appealed to her. On the map the dark line of the Rio Grande looked like a large river. In truth, to her disappointment it was more of a trickle — about ankle deep in a lot of places.

Rising in the middle of the city, the Franklin Mountains divided the west and east parts of town. They seemed but hills compared to the glacier-covered mountains of her home state. But the night stars of the desert sky were so beautiful! And the sunsets spectacular, especially if there were some clouds. Since few trees obscured the view, the sky panorama was enormous.

She liked getting to know her roommates in the dorm. They ate together in the cafeteria. She met a friend, Allie, who was adventurous and liked to shop with her in Juarez, Mexico. They took the bus downtown and walked across the border. They found unusual gifts among the many booths. Crossing back to the United States from there just took the statement, "American".

Once, they rode the bus into the city of Chihuahua and toured an old church and a museum dedicated to the life of the folk-hero, Pancho Villa—who had been murdered in 1923.

In December everyone at school looked forward to the Christmas break. Desert weather was temperamental. In the middle of the month snow began to fall and excitement percolated throughout the dorm. It kept snowing. That day at lunch she met Simon. He introduced himself and sat at her table. He piqued her curiosity with his upbeat attitude. He could talk about just anything and round it back to what he wanted them to know.

Before she knew it, they were walking in the snow. She wore a warm coat, noticed he had a light one but didn't seem to feel the cold. They walked about the campus. It was beautiful! The snow was now knee-deep and no one knew how to drive in it.

The schools closed. That evening she tried to get a ticket to return home and found the planes were not running...too much snow to clear the runway. There was almost never any use for snowplows in El Paso.

She walked down to the train station and Simon went with her. No tickets were available here, either. With the Vietnam War going on soldiers had priority and all spots were filled. A day later she went to the bus station and waited in line to get on a Greyhound headed west to Phoenix and from there the roads were clear. Two days traveling and she was home!

In Edmonds, the rain clouds darkened the sky most of the time and the sun was not visible. She skied in the mountains with her family. Together they decorated a freshly-cut Christmas tree which her Dad, Harold, had brought home. Her mother, Gina, cooked her famous oyster bisque soup for Christmas Eve. They attended church service early on Christmas Day and went home to open presents.

Soon it was time to return. The bright sun hit her as she descended from the plane and she noted the sun did not appear once in Edmonds, that whole vacation.

In the springtime she and Simon had fun climbing in the Franklin Mountains. They tried to fly kites from the peaks and found the downdraft dragged them down. They walked everywhere. She never knew what Simon would say. While she had traveled on family vacations to the National Parks, he had traveled a lot more places while working.

He warned her to never go to his house. He didn't say much about his family but wanted to know about hers. His opinions were unconventional. Once, he told her, he worked for the *Migrant* council in Colorado and decided that the migrants were much better off and had more amenities than his own family. Many drove big new trucks and worked half the year.

In her second year of college Zelene, along with a dozen other girls that shared a kitchen, lived in a rented room of a beautiful old house that had large balconies on the first and second floor. The year was 1968 — the year of the assassination of Martin Luther King, Jr. and Robert Kennedy. It was the time of the Vietnam War and demonstrations and race riots. Boys her age were assigned a draft number and positions were drawn. Those receiving a low number could be drafted and sent to war. Many young men died. Those who returned were not often treated as heroes or thanked for their service.

Occasionally she got letters from Simon who worked in distant states. He returned near Christmas vacation as Zelene was getting ready to go home. Her former roommate, Valerie was going to be driving with a friend to her home in Reno and asked if Zelene wanted to share the ride that far. Zelene came into the dorm room as Valerie was packing.

"Look at what I made for my sister! And my brother-in-law!" She held up colorfully crocheted items. "They'll be surprised!" She wrapped them up in bright red and green paper and tied bows onto them.

"They don't know Robert is giving me a ride. I think I'll get a sheet and appear at their window! They'll think it's a ghost."

Valerie was always lively and cheerful!

"Simon's back in town."

"He is? Why don't we bring him along?"

"Ha! That would be funny! He might like meeting my family." Zelene added, not taking Valerie seriously.

"Yes, let's kidnap him!" She laughed.

"I guess I could ask him." Zelene added.

27

Simon

I was broke but liked the idea of being kidnapped. I knew that if it didn't work out I was able to get a job wherever I ended up and make my way back as I had from around the country.

I went home to tell my mother I was leaving again. She yelled at me.

"No, don't go! I have a feeling something is wrong. It is dangerous."

"But, Mom, I already told her I'll go. It won't be for long." I reassured her.

My mother frowned at me as she ironed. "I can't shake this feeling. I don't think you should go, son."

"I already agreed. They will wait for me. Do I have any clean clothes?"

"Here...some new underwear. Take these." She handed me a sack.

"Adiós. I love you, Mom."

"Okay. Be careful. *Que Diós te bendiga!*"

Then, I took the little sack and went out to the desert to think. A week before I had had a dream about a car accident. In this dream, some people died and I ended up with little more than a few scratches. Together with my mother's premonition was this dream a warning? I wasn't sure.

I shook off the thoughts. I already said that I would go. It was exciting and I liked adventure. I wanted to meet Zelene's family. I wasn't sure what they would think of *me*.

We started late in the morning when Robert drove to pick us up. Zelene wanted to help drive but since she had never driven a stick shift they didn't let her. Although I had been driving for years I had never got a license. Valerie and Robert were sure of the way, and confident. The roads were clear and easy to drive in the day time. Country music streamed from the radio. We were happy to be travelling together.

As we left Phoenix and turned off the main highway at Wickenberg, the sun hung low in the sky. Suddenly it was much colder as we moved up the mountains on a shortcut—highway 93. Darkness fell quickly. We could see patches of snow alongside the road. I put my arm around Zelene and pulled her next to me. She snuggled close. It was nice and warm in the car but very cold outside.

Valerie drove carefully along the winding mountainous highway. All of a sudden I could feel the car slipping.

"Watch out! Valerie!" Robert yelled.

The car twisted sideways and we were skidding headfirst into the ditch alongside the road. Brakes were useless with no traction on the ice patch. Before we hit the side of the mountain the car swung in the opposite direction and I felt that we were falling, tumbling off the side of the cliff.

For a while all was blank...When I came to I heard a hissing sound. I found myself inside the car alone. A door was torn off. I scrambled out and called everyone's names. *Zelene! Valerie! Robert!* There was no answer.

Maybe they all got out and left me alone in the car.

I looked around and saw no one. It was very, very cold. A long ways above me was the faint outline of the road. I was on a steep rockslide. With only dim starlight I crawled up among the boulders. It was a long way to the road.

I kept calling their names. No answer. There was no one there! No cars came. I saw no headlights anywhere. I thought maybe that I was dreaming. I only wore a tee shirt and my body shook in the cold. I decided it wasn't a dream, as I shivered.

I had to find them. With my heart pounding, I made my way back down the boulders as quickly as I could. It was then that I heard whimpering. I was overjoyed to find Zelene sitting on the ground. She looked alright but she just kept glancing around and asking, "Where's my shoe?" I kissed her on the top of her head and told her not to worry—that I'd find her shoe.

A ways from her I found Robert. He was not moving. I knew *he* was not going to make it. There was no sign of Valerie anywhere.

I had to get help. It was so cold it was hard to move. I stumbled upon a sleeping bag near the car. I rolled it a ways down the hill into a slight gully, then, I carried Zelene down. I unrolled the bag and put her inside it.

We would all be dead if I didn't get help. I clawed my way back up the steep rockslide and stood on the road. It was still totally dark. No cars, no lights, no sounds. I looked up at the sky and prayed for strength. Now stars began appearing, filling the sky with brilliance.

After a long time I saw two lights coming from a long ways away. I decided I was going to stand in the middle of the road. If they hit me, they hit me, but they were going to have to stop.

It seemed like ages before a car slowed as it approached and an elderly white man looked at me warily. I know I must have surprised him....I was alone, in the dark, brown-skinned, dressed in a tee shirt in the mountains in the freezing cold. He rolled his window down slightly.

"There's been an accident! The car went off the road." I told him, shaking in the cold. There was a woman with the man.

"I can't see anything." He said suspiciously.

"You can't see unless you go to the side of the road." *He had to believe me!*

He stared at me, unsure of the situation, then another car pulled up behind him. Inside, there were another man and woman. The men got out of the cars and shone a flashlight down the hillside. Now, far below, the metal of the smashed car reflected their light. They could see clothes strewn around it.

"You have to help them! There are three more people down there!" I begged them, urgently.

The men talked together and decided the women would drive in to call the state patrol for help and they would stay. The women drove away and I waited so I could lead them down.

Then more people started to show up...Indian Affairs Police from Wikieup, State Troopers, sheriffs. I took them down to find Zelene still in the sleeping bag in a dazed state.

It did not take long before they found Robert's body. They asked me again and again, "Who was in the car?"

I gave them the names and what I knew of the addresses.

"Are you sure?" They searched and searched but they couldn't find Valerie.

A group arrived with a stretcher to bring Zelene up to the highway and into an ambulance.

Suddenly I was exhausted. I sat on a rock to rest. It was out of my hands.

At last they discovered Valerie. She was beneath the car...she had died instantly. Then, they took me in a car to the hospital in Kingman.

I awoke the next day to see above me a man in white jacket with a stethoscope around his neck.

"You are a very lucky young man!" The doctor told me. "All you have is a little glass in your leg, and that isn't doing any harm — it can just stay there."

"Where's Zelene? Is she okay?"

"She has a concussion but I think she's going to be all right." He reassured me. "She's in the room next door."

I saw a wheel chair in the room. "Do you mind if I use this?"

"No, go right ahead."

As soon as he left the room I sat in the wheel chair and propelled it down the hallway with my hands. I looked through the open door of the next room. Zelene lay back in the hospital bed. Her head was wrapped in bandages. She smiled at me as I rolled to her side. I was relieved to see she was all right. Then I heard a voice down the hallway.

"Where's my daughter?"

"It must be your mother," I said as I tried to wheel out of the room.

"How did she get here?" Zelene was puzzled.

A white-haired lady tried to enter and shoved me back inside the room and out of the doorway, in her eagerness to get in.

"There you are!"

"Hi, Mom, this is Simon."

"Oh, he's cute," she snapped, glancing at me and then quickly turning back to appraise her daughter's condition.

I rolled into the hallway, left the wheel chair and went to wait in the lobby. I took a deep breath and exhaled. Zelene was going to be okay. Seeing that with my own eyes helped the tension leave my body.

After a while Zelene's mother, Gina, came out and started interrogating me.

"Where are you going?"

"Back to El Paso, I guess."

"Do you have your ticket?"

"Not yet."

"Will you go with me to get her things this afternoon?"

"Sure. I'll wait for you." I went outside the hospital and lit a cigarette.

126

Later, Gina found me and we walked to her rental car. I got uneasily into the passenger seat.

"This is just like an airplane. Extinguish your cigarette and fasten your seat belt." She announced.

I had just been in an accident in which two people were killed. I clenched my fists as we went careening down the road to the wrecking yard that held the car. I could feel my heart beating fast.

Suddenly she slammed on the brakes and I let out a cry. She pointed ahead. "There's a car up there, turning."

I looked up the roadway and saw a car a quarter of a mile away. As soon as it turned she was once again speeding along.

When we got to the wrecking yard we saw a pile of clothes and other items. Gina found her daughter's suitcase and a few familiar things. She turned to me.

"Where's *your* suitcase?"

"I didn't bring one." I brushed it off lightly.

"Well, didn't you bring anything?" She drilled me.

"Yes, there it is—underwear." I picked up my paper bag from the pile and looked inside. They were still in the package.

Gina bought my bus ticket. Now, that Zelene's mother was taking her to the airport I was ready to say goodbye.

Zelene sat in the car, listlessly. I went over to give her a kiss. Before I could reach her, the door was slammed shut in my face.

"Goodbye." I watched the car disappear down the road.

Although I was still shaken up, I was going to recall that Zelene's very forthright, take-charge mother had called *me*, Simon Palomar, "cute".

Before I arrived home news of the accident had spread. People knew that two people in the car had been killed and many wondered if I had been one of them.

As I walked down the street I was often greeted with these words: "You're alive! Thank God! I thought you were dead."

28

Two Weddings

When Zelene returned to college in the fall, she rented, with a roommate, an apartment close to school and enjoyed cooking for herself and others. She was grateful for many kind friends who liked to get together. She tried not to think too much of the accident—she felt so bad for Valerie's family. She didn't know why she only suffered a concussion and the other two were dead. If Simon hadn't come along with them, they would all have died and no one would have found the car for weeks.

Now he was gone to other states, working a lot of the time. The pace of life in El Paso was slower and friendlier. Not sure of a major, she took an eclectic mix of subjects—astronomy, calculus, botany, Russian literature.

She wasn't much of a talker but liked to listen to the different accents here—the East Texas drawl, the English/Spanish mix, the cowboy anecdotes. Some friends played the guitar and sang. The folk musicians, Bob Dylan and Joan Baez, were popular.

Probably the best storyteller was Simon. She didn't know whether he was kidding half the time. He knew how to make her laugh. He told her that when he was in Dallas working, building houses, there was a very tall man who came with them from deep in Mexico. They called him "The Bird" because he filled a sink with water, stripped off his clothes and then folded himself into it to take his baths. She and Simon wrote letters but they were intermittent and nothing was sure. When he appeared in town they would sometimes see a movie. The clear night skies were magical with so many bright stars.

This evening she was at her apartment when the phone rang and disrupted her studies. Her sister was on the line when she picked up the phone. "Zelene, I'm sorry to tell you this."

"Tell me what? What happened?"

"Buzz was run over by a car last night."

"Oh, no! Did he die?"

"We took him to the vet but he was too far gone. I'm so sorry."

At this point Zelene hung up the phone — tears running down her face. Buzz was her favorite cat of all time. He had been with her through her teen years, ready to jump on her lap and purr loudly any time she needed him. He loved to have his chin rubbed but sometimes would scratch a person if they stopped petting him. He was gray and white and huge. He didn't bond well with others in the family. He had been her special pet. She had other cats before but they didn't have the same personality.

It was silly to cry but she would miss him. She didn't feel like fixing any dinner.

Someone was at the door. She wiped the tears from her face and opened it.

"Simon! Come in." He was dressed in black and wore a *zorro*-style hat.

"What's wrong? Why are you crying?"

"It's nothing." She turned her face away. She didn't want to admit she was crying over a cat.

She could see he wanted to cheer her up. The next sentence completely surprised her.

"Do you want to get married?" He smiled.

"What?"

"Yes, we could go over to Juarez and get married."

It must be one of his jokes. It sounded fun. Just the idea took her mind off her cat. He didn't really mean it but she wasn't going to be the one to back down. "Okay." She laughed. She would call his bluff.

"Get ready. We'll go in a little while."

What should she wear? It was a cold night. She looked in her closet. She selected a red wool suit that her sister had bought while studying in England and sent to her last year. She came out into the living room, smiling.

Simon's head was down, poking through his wallet. "Wait a minute. I don't have the money right now."

Ha! He was already backing out. Then her roommate came in the door.

"What's happening? Zelene, why are you dressed in that nice suit? Are you going somewhere?" Tisha asked.

"We were going to get married tonight but Simon doesn't have the money." She joked.

131

"Are you serious? But *I* do. Simon, I'll lend it to you. How much do you need?" She didn't want to miss out on the excitement.

Simon thought seriously then said, "I'm pretty sure if you lend me forty-five dollars it will be enough. I'll pay you back tomorrow."

Zelene looked outside. It was already dark and late. How far was Simon going to carry this? No office would be open.

"Okay! Can I go with you guys? I'll be your witness."

"Good." Simon answered. "Thanks."

Fifteen minutes later they walked across the Santa Fe Street Bridge into downtown Juarez, Mexico. Vendors assaulted them from all sides.

"Ya want a taxi?" "Buy some flowers for the lady?"

"Do you want to go to the market?"

"Wanna get married?"

"Wanna divorce, mister?"

"See a show?"

"Yes, we want to get married." Simon told one taxi driver.

"Get in, get in." He opened both back doors — happy to have customers. His thick black hair stuck out of his cap. The three of them got in.

Bright lights lit the shops and night-life traffic flowed in the streets and along the sidewalks. Bars opened at all hours, here. The taxi driver wound through narrow streets and away from the tourist area. Was it midnight, yet? Surely no marriage office would be open, now. Tisha bounced up and down on the seat.

"Everything will be fine, you'll see! What a crazy idea!" She was beaming.

Simon put his arm around Zelene's shoulders. She wondered when the joke would be up. The taxi-driver pulled into a dark driveway in front of a building that was completely dark. "Just give me a few minutes, okay? I'll be right back. I have to check on something." He popped out of the taxi and they saw him pound on the door. A light went on inside the house. After a while the door opened and they could see the taxi driver speaking to a man in a bathrobe. He nodded his head and the driver returned to the car.

"It will cost a little more because he had to get out of bed. But she is worth it, no?" Simon put money into the driver's outstretched hand and they were ushered inside.

The magistrate asked questions in Spanish and the taxi driver translated. Before she could think clearly she heard herself say, "I do."

With everyone looking at him, Simon did not want to embarrass himself or her. He said, "I do" and they were signing some papers. Tisha served as witness and because two were required, the taxi driver was the other.

Everyone was exhilarated as they headed back across the border. Now the joke was on both of them. And it lasted for a long while.

Three days later I took the city bus to my house. In the kitchen my mother was rolling out a stack of tortillas.

"Mom, I got married."

She turned her head towards me. "Ha! You're always joking."

"No. Really, I did!"

"Do you really expect me to believe it? To whom?"

"Zelene. I brought the marriage certificate just because I knew you wouldn't believe it." I pulled out a paper from an envelope and spread it before her.

Angela stopped rolling and wiped her floured hands on a towel. "Zelene? That white girl from the college?" She examined the paper I held out. Then she put her hands over her face.

"Yes."

"Well, then, now you are flour from a different sack." She shook open a paper bag and went around the house gathering my clothes, folding them and putting them inside. She handed it to me, anger and sadness in her eyes.

There was not a bit of congratulations from her and I did not expect any.

On the other hand, Zelene waited three days before calling home. She didn't like to tell her mother anything, because she had extreme reactions. And it was her mother who picked up the phone.

"Mom, I don't want to shock you or anything but Simon and I just got married."

"Nooo!" She heard her mother shrieking hysterically. "Harold, your daughter is on the phone."

Then, her father was on the other end, speaking calmly. "Oh, so what do you want? A brass band?" It was his usual dry sense of humor.

"Oh, Dad. I'm fine. Do you want to talk to Simon?"

"Certainly."

She handed the phone to Simon and he talked to his new son-in-law for a few minutes.

The next day they called back in a much calmer manner. Zelene's mother was very concerned they weren't married by a priest.

Gina was a very strong Catholic. She could not understand why Zelene wasn't following the faith in which she had been brought up. She had nightmares of Zelene now burning in hell because she had not received the sacrament of matrimony in the Church. As far as she was concerned, Simon and Zelene were "living in sin". She made this known to them in many ways—especially through phone calls.

I thought about this and we arranged to go to a little Catholic church in El Paso and talk to a priest. We decided it wouldn't hurt to get married to each other again. I wanted peace.

The priest agreed to see us. He wanted to see our baptismal certificates. He talked to us about the seriousness of being married.

"Simon, you know the girls wear these short skirts nowadays. I've found the best way to avoid trouble is to look in another direction." He looked at me seriously, making sure I understood.

I began to feel defensive and nervous and lit a cigarette. We were sitting in his office. After a while I got to the end of it. I saw no ash tray on the desk so I placed the butt on tile floor and squished it with my boot. Father La Pierre stared at me in alarm.

"Now that is something you can not do anymore. You must have consideration for the house and the housekeeper."

"But Father La Pierre, you had no ashtray. I didn't want to start a fire." I was defensive.

I remember all his advice.

A month after our first wedding we took our vows in the church. Zelene's friend, Allie came, and I asked my *padrinos*, Joe and Martha, to come be the witnesses. That was all. Zelene sewed herself a dress and Allie took a picture of both of us.

No one expected our marriage to last, even so. My mother came to tell Zelene she had taken away her source of support. *Welcome to the family!*

Later, when I got to know my father-in-law, he told me "Thank you".

"Thank me for what?" I wanted to know.

"Getting married in the Church. You just don't know what it was like at my house. Gina was terribly worried you both were going to burn in hell. The difference in the house then and now is like between night and day."

I liked my father-in-law very much.

When their first baby was born, ten months later, Zelene saw Simon's relatives counting out the months on their fingers, then, nodding to each other. "*Sí, salió bién.*" But her own mother flew down and helped her care for her first grandchild. Babies were everything to her and her grandchild was of course, perfect. She took charge and scrubbed their apartment and taught her daughter all the details of caring for a newborn — bathing, changing and feeding.

She brought face masks for protection from germs from visitors and a baby scale to weigh him every day. Simon's laid back relatives were taken aback by her quickness. Then she returned home — sending special things by mail — baby clothes, a stroller, a high chair.

Simon went to work at a construction site. They didn't have a car and didn't want one. They walked and took the bus everywhere. Zelene washed the diapers in the bathtub and hung them on a clothesline in the back of the apartment building. They didn't have much but it was enough. Allie came over and helped her tie-dye the diapers a purple color. They dried quickly in the desert wind.

Zelene could tell that Simon had a very different upbringing from hers. They were just about opposite. But they were both stubborn. Her grandmother on her father's side, whose ancestors had come to Oregon in the 1850's, told her the secret to life was, "Never give up. Don't quit."

It had been difficult at first. Somehow she had finished her classes for the semester. When the baby came she was fascinated by him and loved everything about him, although she was inexperienced in baby care.

Simon started to come home from work and drink or not come home at all. He became moody and cried about the past. She worried, waiting, wondering if he was in trouble. She loved Simon but feared he loved drinking more. Alcohol was eating up the money and about everything he did. She considered the possibilities, and was just thinking of how to leave with the baby when he checked himself into an alcohol treatment program. He had just turned twenty-one.

29

Edmonds (1977)

I wrapped a woolen scarf around my neck and pulled down my black stocking cap as I walked out onto the Edmonds fishing pier. I carried my saltwater pole and tackle box in one hand and a white bucket in the other. In Puget Sound the tide was coming in rapidly. Small whitecaps crowned the lines of waves rolling into shore. It would be a full moon tonight even though we might not see it at all above the thick clouds.

I found a spot along the railing that gave me enough room to cast and baited my hook with the small herring that I carried in the bucket. I swung the pole back and released the line while I brought it forward — sending the bait and sinker far out into the water. As I reeled it in with jerking motions, willing the salmon onto my line, I considered how different this kind of fishing was to pole fishing for catfish in the Rio Grande.

Fisherman everywhere are men of hope, I decided...gamblers betting on the next cast of the line, the next bite will be the big one. It was that kind of hope that had given me the courage to marry Zelene and now brought me to Washington with my wife and children. I never wanted to leave. Here the rains fell and snow topped the mountains. I could hike on trails, fish in streams or the ocean. It was beautifully green — not dusty.

I held a good job and was building my own house on a city lot with tall fir and pine trees. Before I put in the walls I was going to have to bring down some of them. El Paso trees never grew to even half the height of these trees — but I had learned how to fell them. I had my own chain saw.

If the stress of building a house didn't drive me back to drinking I must be well on my way to recovery. It had been over a year of sobriety and already it seemed like a lifetime ago that I had gone a second time to rehab. The first time was the year I turned twenty-one — just the age for others to start drinking. No one thought that I could make it. Sometimes I thought I quit just in order to prove wrong those who said I never would. But no — I quit for myself — I wanted to see my own kids grow up in a better way than I had. I tried to be a better father than my own.

Fishing carries a great opportunity for reflection and for planning. Tomorrow my mother and brother were supposed to arrive on the bus — taking the forty-eight hour trip because my mother absolutely refused to even think about flying. This would be the first time I would see them in many years. I'd left responsibilities to my younger brother Nate when I moved.

From his early teens Nate had lived with friends with families that worked with horses. They had discovered that he had an amazing rapport with animals. They took advantage of this, along with his wiry build and light weight and trained him to ride thoroughbreds at the racetrack. He learned quickly and worked hard.

From the day that I went to his school and signed him out at the age of fifteen he had ridden as a jockey. First, he rode as an apprentice, with a five pound weight allowance, then as a regular jockey. He won over and over! He moved quickly to the top of the standings.

It was a very dangerous profession but he could make more money in a few minutes than the rest of us in weeks. He would take a horse with long odds and trail around the backstretch until they rounded the last curve and then Nate sent his horse flying.

I enjoyed having Zelene's parents and brother and sister live nearby. They made me feel welcome all the time. They invited us over and loved babysitting the grandchildren. Zelene's family all graduated from college and went beyond.

That's where we met—in college. At first I had struggled—coming from so far behind with a GED and almost no high school. I ran into elementary teachers who told me "I knew you had it in you."

I wanted to reply, "No, you didn't!" But instead I answered, "Really?" and went on to class.

Suddenly, my pole bent down. Could it be a salmon? Something was yanking hard on the line. I got hold of the reel and wound it in when it went slack and let it play when the fish pulled the bait. Other fishermen saw the pole bending and came to see. Some of them threw their lines in nearby.

"Give him room. He's got a big one coming," yelled the man fishing to my right.

My pole bounced up and down as the fish tried to throw off the hook. I knew it was too big to pull up to the top of the pier. I had to lead it in closer to shore where the pier ran closer to the level of the water.

"Coming through!" I called as I moved with my pole and other fishermen pulled in their lines to let me by. The fish was now tiring. I pulled it up into a waiting net. A king salmon—almost ten pounds!

"What a beauty!" A man admired the fish. I pictured Zelene's smiling face when I brought it home.

The next day my mother and Nate were the first ones to descend the stairs of the bus when it pulled into the depot in downtown Seattle. It had been several years since we had seen each other. I had last been in El Paso for funerals. My nephew had died of leukemia a few days before Christmas. That was too much for my sister Martha's heart. Earlier that year she had lost her oldest daughter and now her son. She died of a heart attack on Christmas Eve.

I'd come but it was all a blur. I saw everything through the haze of alcohol and tears. What a sad time. I ended up drinking so much that I started to spit up blood. When I returned I'd agreed to go to rehab.

"*Hijo!*" exclaimed my mother. Her face told me she appreciated seeing me alive and sober. She hugged me and I shook hands with Nate. We drove back to the house in which we were living while I built my own. Two more grandchildren she hadn't met were there along with the oldest two born in Texas.

The kids struggled to understand what was said because everyone was speaking Spanish. Zelene had cooked a pot of stew and the travelers were happy to sleep after their two day trip.

The next morning the weather was sunny and the sky clear. Zelene's mother, Gina drove over to meet them.

"Angela, I'd like to take you to see the sights. Would you like to go to the Public Market?" Gina rocked on her feet from heels to toes in her eagerness to get started.

She nodded her head.

"Let's go then!" Gina's movements were always quick. Everything she did was still rapid even though she was in her sixties.

Angela spoke to her in broken English. She wasn't sure what was going to happen but she was used to the public markets of Juarez. Driving in a car was a different matter.

In a few hours they returned. Angela carried a grocery bag. Her eyes were huge and her face was pale. After my mother-in-law left I asked her, "Mom, did you like the Public Market?"

"Simon, never let me go with her again!" she yelled in Spanish. Her legs shook and she sat down.

"Where did you go?"

"I don't know where it was that she took me after the market. The road went across the water and there were waves coming up the sides. She drives so fast and all the while she was talking and pointing at some white mountains at the same time. I was so frightened! I thought we were going to drown in the water and I didn't want to look up. It was moving and it made me sick to see it."

"That sounds like the bridge across Lake Washington. Didn't you tell her to take you back?"

"She did! Across the water the same way! She drives crazy."

"Did you get to the Public Market?" I wanted to know.

She pointed to the bag. "Yes, they had things to make *menudo*. Oh, the flowers there are beautiful. But, I never want to ride with her again!"

I chuckled. I knew my mother-in-law drove like a race car driver. I couldn't tell her "no, don't take her." My mother wasn't used to much more water than what the Rio Grande held when irrigation season came around. She even got seasick looking at the moving expanse of lake water.

"Mom, and you were afraid to fly in an airplane!"

30

.

Return (Years Later)

The green station wagon was loaded with my wife and kids and camping gear as we approached the end of our nearly 2,000 mile drive to El Paso. It had been fifteen years since I lived there. I tried to picture my old adobe house. The summer sun beat down on us and we rolled down all the windows and wet towels to cool us as we came near.

We reached Texas and it was just five miles more to the edge of town. I turned onto Cameo Street. There was a big grocery store and houses built close together. The city had grown out and filled in my old neighborhood. I looked for my old house and wondered how much change I would find when I got there.

I pulled the car into the sandy front yard and looked around. It was as if time had stood still here. The same tree stood in the front yard. The water spigot was near it. There was no other foliage anywhere. The screen door had a big rip in it and swung on a broken hinge. A pillow blocked the air from a broken window. The same outhouse stood in the rear—looking weatherworn and filthy with much use. In its early heyday—as a double-seater it had been somewhat of a Cadillac of an outhouse. The same Maytag wringer washer stood sideways and off balance near the house.

I remembered with regret the promise I had made to my mother years ago. "Someday I'm going to build you a real house."

I honked the horn as we swung open the car doors.

"We're here!" I told the kids as a cloud of flies greeted us.

"Where?" They asked, finding it hard to believe anyone lived in this tiny broken shack.

But it was certain that they did. In fact, I found it was overflowing with people who staked claims to spots on the beds or floor.

"Right here. My old home." I didn't say any more but honked the horn again.

"This is a house?" Tim asked.

I had told the kids so many stories about this place—now, in front this shack—they couldn't imagine anyone living here. And out poured many people—including my mother.

"Kids, this is your *abuela,* your grandmother."

They climbed out of the car to greet her. At the same time a roly-poly man in a baseball cap flew out the back and clambered over a rock wall and disappeared. A chorus of barking dogs marked his path. A woman with tattoos on her muscled arms pointed at him and bent down in laughter.

"He saw your green wagon and took off. He thinks you're the *migra*."

"Who is *he*?"

"That's Lily's man," someone hooted.

"Kids, this is your *Tia* Lily, my big sister," I introduced the wild-looking tattooed woman who came up and grabbed me.

The small cement porch in the front smelled strongly of urine.

"Hey, weren't they even able to make it to the outhouse?"

The afternoon sun beat down and flies settled on everything and we swatted at them.

People streamed around us, some carrying babies. There were small kids I had never seen. Everyone was yelling and jabbering at once. My own kids looked a little bewildered. They didn't understand much Spanish.

Everything had gone downhill and was far worse than I had imagined, from another state.

Word spread quickly in the neighborhood and more and more people came. I didn't know half the people that were there. One of my sisters pointed out her kids. I told her the names of my own.

My mother still liked to feed people. I helped her lay an old wooden door on two chunks of wood to use as an outdoor table. She asked a friend to bring out a steaming pot from inside the house and sent a boy with a small booklet to a store a block away to get some tortillas.

"You don't make your tortillas anymore, Mom?"

"No, not much. Now we have *estampillas*," She announced proudly.

"Ooh! I came all this way and none of your own tortillas." I teased.

"Maybe later. Not today!"

Inside, a radio played *ranchera* music so loudly that the sounds flowed out of the house and it was necessary to almost yell to be heard.

We were soon sitting down on upended buckets and broken folding chairs to bowls of her wonderful *menudo*. The kids looked for some eating utensils. Here, they often used tortillas as silverware but for soups a spoon was needed.

"Do you have spoons?" I asked my sister Vela. She just stood there and laughed.

"Yes, I'll get them." Carla, my youngest sister went inside and came back out with five mismatched spoons.

"Ha! They don't know how to eat with tortillas!" Their cousins mocked.

"Hey, leave them alone. They'll learn." I was proud of my own children. They were all very smart and did well in school.

Some of them, but not all, liked *menudo*, though. I didn't want my mother to feel bad, but I could see the small dog by their feet was getting fed.

"How about some *chile*?" My mother's deep red, poisonous-looking *chile* stood as some of the world's hottest and she loved it that way.

"Okay. Okay." Zach and Inez each had a small spoonful mixed into the broth. With one sip of it they started to hiccup and choke.

"Water! Water!" they cried, their faces turning a bright red to the entertainment of the natives.

A girl went to the spigot and brought two mayonnaise jars filled with water. They drank them quickly but I could see their mouths were still burning. I'd forgotten how everyone laughed at the others' pain here.

"Try a little salt." They shook a little salt on their hands and licked it. That provided some relief. Others slurped up the remainder in the pot with great relish.

Car after car drove up into the yard. Men I recognized unloaded an ice chest with beer and soon offered me one.

"No thanks, I don't drink." I informed them.

"The hell you don't!" They stood next to me and popped the tops of their cans. The familiar smell of beer wafted in the air. "Here, take one!" Omar held it in front of me.

I had waited a long time to come back and for a good reason. In my younger days I drank more by far than many people do in their lifetime. I was barely twenty-one when I first went to a hospital for alcoholism. In that time, people considered excessive drinking a character weakness—a psychological disorder. They gave me *antabuse*—a pill that causes you to get violently ill if you take a drink. I also learned it can damage the liver. Another medication that I was prescribed I soon quit taking because it slowed me down and made me sleepy.

I quit drinking for a time but I found out some people who say they're your friends really can't stand to see you quit drinking when *they* still do. I was never offered so many drinks as when I quit. They wanted me to fail.

It had taken a move far away and another rehab where I learned about nutrition and chemical addiction and heredity. I now had more than ten years of sobriety behind me and I felt good!

"There's more to life than drinking! All those cans that were going to be mine, you can have them," I told them.

"Hey, if Simon can give it up, so can you!" Omar's wife yelled. Omar glared at me as he guzzled his beer.

My old friends were angry. I had a new role. I disrupted their easy life where they lived to gather and drink. Most of them didn't imagine life without beer.

Now I could hear the mothers and wives of old friends telling them, "*Mira, el no toma!* Why can't you be like him! He doesn't drink." The tension began.

"Omar, tell them where your car is now." His wife came over to my side. "The idiot! Another DWI and they towed the car."

"So—you think you're better than us now." He staggered over closer, his beer clenched in his fist.

"No. But it costs a lot to drink and I find it's a lot more fun to watch others make fools of themselves than to do it myself."

As an ancient truck with many dents rattled into the yard, I recognized the driver—Victor, *El Mariachi*, another old drinking buddy. The tires were so bald that pieces of the wires stuck through the rubber.

"Victor, you'd better watch out for the mosquitoes!" I told him as he got out, reaching his hand out to me.

"Why's that?"

"If they bite your tires you'll be riding on rims."

He wore his usual cowboy hat and boots. From the bed of the truck he brought out a tub full of deep-fried turkey tails—enough for everybody! We traded more insults and laughed about the past. As the sun went down we built a fire and sat around. He took out his guitar and strummed. I joined in singing *corridas* - story-telling songs in Spanish. Many were sad songs of the days of Pancho Villa.

I wanted my wife and kids to avoid the expected drunken rowdiness, so, I accepted the offer of my kind cousin—a place to stay at her home. We left for the night.

31

The next day as we returned to the house a long-haired bearded man staggered out from under a nearby mulberry tree. Stacks of aluminum cans clanked behind him as he moved out from his nest.

"Hey, hey, Mama! Feed your baby bird!" He flapped his arms and smiled broadly showing his teeth. His mustache was streaked with silver paint. I squinted to get a better look. Was this my little brother? When we moved away, he had been a good student in middle school, getting along with everyone, even the teacher. What had happened? My mother had always protected him.

"Hey, Bro!" He lumbered toward us gathered next to the house.

"Kids, this is your Uncle Billy." An overpowering chemical smell surrounded him as he neared. Could he be dangerously high?

"Go away, Billy." I didn't want him to get too near to my kids.

"I'm hungry! Feed your baby bird!" He yelled louder, laughing and flapping his arms again.

The kids thought he was entertaining them.

"Billy!" My mother opened the screen and called to him, smiling at her favorite. She disappeared into the house then emerged and handed him a large bean burrito. He grabbed it, nodding his thanks and retreated to the tree.

The sun already beat down on us. We stood under the other tree. My mother brought out a pile of papers for me to look at.

"I don't know what has happened. They haven't sent me the property tax for a few years and I think there is trouble with it." She always wanted me to take care of papers, etc.

"Why? Did you sign something?" She looked at me carefully, sizing up my expression. She only let me know what she wanted me to know or had to let me know.

"You know Billy. He's had some trouble with the law. One time they held him in the jail—it was going to be for a long time. I bailed him out. He promised he would stay out of trouble from then on. He stays close, now."

"You bailed him out? How?" I watched her face.

"You know. I didn't have money to put up. I went to SSS Bail Bonds."

"What did they want?" I was worried.

"They told me give them so much a month."

"Mom, did you sign anything?"

She gazed at Billy who was enjoying his burrito. "Well, I had to bring the deed to the house," she said quietly.

"WHAT!" I yelled. "You traded in the house for him?"

"No, no." She tried to quiet me. "I paid it! I signed a paper and I had to go to town every month and pay it. It is all paid. But they wouldn't give me the deed. They said they couldn't do it."

"Why not? Do you have the receipts?"

"Yes, I have the contract. I kept the receipts. Here, look in this." She rustled through the stack and handed me a large business envelope stuffed with papers.

I started plowing through the papers. From all that I could tell she had paid SSS Bonds for years. But what had happened? There it was! The last receipt showing nothing owed.

That same day I drove downtown and found the tax office to find out why she had not got a tax bill in years. I waited in line for thirty minutes before finding out I had to go to another area. Another line — twenty more minutes. I filled out paperwork that included the address and after a while an older lady, with reading glasses hanging from a silver chain called me to the desk.

"This property tax has not been paid in years. The property is about to go up for auction because of delinquent taxes. The current amount with penalties is approximately $948 dollars."

"But whose name is on the property? My mother owns it and lives there but no longer receives the tax statement although she paid it for years."

She scrutinized the paper. "It is under the name of P. E. Garza."

"How did that happen? I know at one time she signed it over to a bail bondsman; but she paid it in full. I have the paper to show. I can show you."

"I'm not sure. Let me check the address to which the tax statement is sent." Her heels clicked with authority as she disappeared into the hall that led into a labyrinth of county files.

After another long while she was back at the desk and motioning to me. "You'll have to come back tomorrow. I need to check on some things."

"I will be here tomorrow!" *Great! My mother might lose her house and I had to wait another day.* I kicked the door as I left.

32

At the house I found Zelene talking to my sisters in the yard and the younger kids playing in the sand and a tub of water. A lot of other people were milling around even though it was Thursday. I didn't see Billy.

"Does anybody here work?" I was surprised so many people lived in the house.

"Ha, ha!" My sisters laughed. I found out they all waited for the mail. Food stamps would come. They had welfare for the children. What more did they need. They sold food stamps to get extra money. Their men didn't work but they needed beer and cigarettes. Everyone knew how to game the system!

"Who stays at the house?" No one answered me. They looked from one to another. My youngest sister had a baby at a young age, and my mother cared for her as her own. What a tangled web! The ones who stayed at the house were the ones that needed to at the moment—those who were thrown out of the public housing or hadn't paid rent. It was still a matter of getting there first at night. My mother found it difficult to deny anyone a place—after all it was not a palace.

Men started arriving with cases of beer. Here they were not chased away.

"Hi, Donny." I recognized a neighbor of old. He was dressed in slacks and a white shirt.

"Dad, is that him? Is that the guy that pooped in his pants." My son asked, recognizing the name.

I had told many stories of my home and neighbors as the kids were growing up. Now, that they met them in person, I could see this might embarrass people. As a boy, Donny pooped in his pants on his way home from school. That story and all its details was one such tale that Ken found very entertaining. He wanted to hear it over and over and laughed every time. I nodded to him while motioning him with my hand to hold it down.

Ken seldom held back. He roared with laughter as he watched Donny. He was a real person!

"That didn't happen!" Donny had heard him and denied it all with an angry face.

This just made Ken laugh the more and point him out to his brothers. The stories were true!

"They built a nice park nearby." Zelene redirected the conversation. "The kids can play over there for a while."

"Go ahead." I agreed. Their cousins walked them over to a lush green park with a government housing complex nearby.

I went inside the house to tell my mother what I discovered in town.

In a few minutes the kids came back with unhappy faces.

"What happened?" Zelene asked. The answer was a combined effort.

"We were playing tag in the park...just running around. Other kids were playing ball. The ball disappeared and so did our cousins."

"Then a police car drove up. A policeman came up to us. He wanted to know our names."

"We told him our first names."

"But, he wanted to know our last name. When we told him 'Palomar' , he said, 'No Palomars allowed in the park.' We had to leave."

"He told us to get out of there. Why, Dad?"

I glanced at the group of people now gathered under the shade of the elm tree.

"Lily drank too much last night. There was a fight at the park. I think she knocked someone's tooth out." Donny told me. "Billy gets goofy and they are afraid of him, too."

"My kids aren't troublemakers." I put in. "They are good kids. It's not fair to them."

"Yes, but it's *your* last name."

On Friday I drove back downtown, parked and put money into the meter. I hoped it wouldn't be another long wait. City officials never seemed to hurry. This day the line was shorter. I talked to several other people before the lady to whom I had spoken previously called my name. I went to her desk.

She held a piece of paper in front of me. "The name on the property, P. E. Garza, shows the same address as SSS Bonds."

"But my mother paid them. Why isn't it in her name?"

"There was a lien on it. No one paid the taxes for five years, so it is getting ready to go for auction. I'm sure these people knew that. It shows up as undeveloped property. It could go for a song."

"What can I do?"

"She needs to get the property back in her name. I would go see the people at SSS Bonds, if I were her."

"Do you have the address?"

She wrote it down on a piece of paper and handed to me.

"Thank you!" I nodded to her and hurried out of the building.

SSS Bonds was located a block away from the downtown jail so I walked on over. I pushed a heavy brass door open and went inside the dark office. I couldn't see anybody within but heard a buzzer go off as the door shut behind me.

In a short while a man in a gray dress shirt and gray tie appeared looked through thick glasses at me from behind the desk. "Hello. Can I help you?"

"I'm looking for Mr. Garza, Mr. P.E. Garza."

"Mr. Garza no longer works here." He replied abruptly.

Then I tried to explain the situation. He listened to me, resting his elbows on the desk top. When I asked him about the property and the fact that my mother had paid it, he shrugged.

"I'd like to help you but we have no records anymore."

"Why not?"

"One day the FBI swarmed in here with a truck, boxed it all up and took it."

"But I have the paper that shows she paid it off." I pulled it out of the envelope and spread it out before him.

He barely glanced at it. "Is that so?" He looked away from me and began ruffling through a pile of envelopes.

I felt the heat building inside me even though the room was air-conditioned. *What more could I do now?*

I hit the desk with my fist. I saw his eyes widen in surprise. "I'm going to find out what's going on and be back." I turned and walked quickly back to my car.

From my cousin's house I called my brother-in-law in Washington State. He was an attorney and I was desperate for advice. After talking to his secretary I soon heard his friendly voice.

"Simon, how are you?"

"Barry, I could be better. I've got some legal questions. I'd like to help my mother keep from losing her house to some crooks." I explained what had happened as quickly as I could.

He asked a few questions. "Let me get back to you in a bit. I 'm busy with a client at the moment, but I will call back." He hung up.

I looked at my watch and waited by the phone.

In a short while he was on the line again. "I looked up the statutes in Texas and I think what you are going to need to do is get what's called a *quit deed* from the bond company. You might have to see a lawyer, there. I don't know how you're going to get someone to sign it but if you have a paper saying it was paid they are in big trouble if they haven't turned the deed back to your mother's name. Let me know what's going on!"

"Thanks, Barry. I'll see what I can do and keep you informed." I hurriedly drove to town. When I reached SSS Bonds' office, I pushed on the door. It wouldn't budge. I couldn't see anything lit inside. I'd have to wait until Monday.

On my way back, I stopped by my mother's. People gathered around in the yard...among them I saw my brother, Billy. He was celebrating with a beer can in his hand.

159

"She paid me." He waved some money bills above his head. "Five hundred dollars."

It was hard to understand what was happening but he was sending people to buy beer.

"Why, Billy?" Someone asked.

"To marry her. Over in Juarez."

"Then, where is your wife?" Friends called to him.

"She gave me the money; then, after we were married, we came across the border and she went away."

"So, now, are you a husband for hire?"

"Yes, that's me—husband for hire. Five hundred dollars!" He proclaimed proudly, in a loud voice. His grin was huge.

I shook my head. I was so angry with him that I couldn't speak. My mother could lose the house because of him and he was still the same.

33

Monday, I started early to town. I parked nearby the entrance and waited in my car to see a woman enter the SSS Bonds office. Before the door could close behind her, I followed her inside. The same man sat behind the desk. I waited until the woman before me paid money and left and then I confronted him.

"Sir, I've spoken to my attorney and he tells me that since my mother paid you, you must sign the house back to her. Either you do that or we will sue you for a lot more than that lot is worth! You decide."

He stared at me through his thick glasses. My mother's English was minimal and I'm sure they thought that she was an easy target for people like this. Her property was a lot more valuable now, for developers, than it used to be. Now, he had to face me or a possible legal suit.

He picked up a pile of papers on the desk, ruffling through them. I waited.

Finally, he looked up at me. "You know, Mr. Palomar, at one time I used to manage this company, so although Mr. Garza is not available, if you can bring me a *quit deed*, my signature will be good."

"Thank you, Mr....?

"Lugo, Juan Lugo."

161

"As soon as I can locate one, I will be back." I needed to hurry before he changed his mind or left.

I headed for the court house. After a lot of run around I was sent to an office that could give me a generic *quit deed*. As I went up and down stairs and elevators, I noticed a bulletin board with a yellow paper. As I examined it, I found it contained a description of a program in the city to rebuild blighted, rundown properties. My mother's certainly fit that description. I copied down the name and the phone number to contact.

Mr. Lugo had no problem signing the deed and stamping it with office initials. Now I knew I must go back to the county office and file it. Then, it would be up to us to pay the back taxes or it still could be lost.

Back home, Billy was sitting on a log under the tree. I thought I needed to collect as much money as possible from those who lived in the house.

"Billy, I wonder if you have anything left from your *husband for hire* adventure? We've got to pay the taxes or lose the house." I stood next to him.

"Sure, Bro, I got it." He reached into his pockets, still in a good humor. "My friends helped me celebrate." He pulled out a couple of dollars from one pocket, and a twenty just about fell out and blew away as he reached into the other pocket. "Here, take it. Do you want a smoke?" He lit a cigarette and took a long puff.

"No, no. I quit that—I call them coffin nails." I grabbed the twenty. "Some friends! They didn't leave you much."

I didn't want to ask my mother for any money, but asked my sisters and brothers that were staying or had stayed there. Each pointed a finger at the other. I collected a little and made up the rest from my savings and returned to the tax office for another long wait before paying. The house was saved—for a while, anyway!

Later, I called the contact person for rebuilding properties. At first the phone rang and rang—no answer. I called back twice, at different times before reaching a secretary.

"You will have to make an appointment and the next available one is in six weeks."

"I have to see him now. I won't be able to come in, then." We were leaving in a week.

"I'm sorry. That's all I can do."

"Where is your office located?" I decided my only hope was to visit in person.

The next day I headed back to town with the record of the tax payment and the clear property deed. I found the housing office and asked to see the man in charge.

The secretary sat behind her desk filing her nails. "Mr. Bulger is not in. He only sees people by appointment."

"That's okay. I'll wait here." I was not going to be dismissed so easily. I sat in one of the chairs and looked at my watch.

"But, he won't be coming in today!" She insisted. "You're wasting your time."

"I'm just going to wait here anyway—until he does." I picked up a magazine and leaned back.

She glared at me. I could tell she wasn't comfortable with me in the reception room.

163

I waited and waited. The secretary answered the phone a couple of times but did little else. After a couple of hours a man in a brown suit with a briefcase came in.

He stared at me then said. "I recognize you! Palomar, Simon, isn't it?" He reached out to shake my hand. "John Bulger. Remember me from high school? Come in. Come right in my office."

He remembered me and I wasn't sure why. I just hoped it wasn't for something bad—no, he was friendly.

"Anything I can help you with?"

Then, I asked about the qualifications for the program for blighted properties. I showed him my mother's papers.

"If she owns the property with a clear title we can look into it." He pulled out a city map and found the address on the street. "The city allots a certain amount of grant money and then the rest is covered with a no-interest loan with a very reasonable monthly payment. I'll give you the application for her."

"Thanks, John. That would be wonderful for her. I'm returning to Washington State but I'll keep in contact from there by phone—she doesn't have one. Here is my number." I wrote it down for him.

"Great! You do that." He shook my hand again as I left.

34

A year later

Angela Palomar blinked her eyes and smiled as she came to look. Yes, it was real. They had started tearing down her old adobe house and hauling it away. Every day something more was done.

First the men dug the foundation and poured the cement. It was level and solid. She watched the walls go up and then the roof framed. Everyone walked through the skeleton of the house—pointing out rooms and planning how to claim a spot.

She wasn't young but she would have some years left to enjoy it. They installed nice glass windows with screens on them—and the door had a screen, too. The flies and mosquitoes would have to stay outside! They let her pick the color of carpet and she chose white—as white as she could get. The walls would be white, too.

Her sister laughed at her. "Why do you want white? You know everybody will track in the dirt and it will be ugly in no time."

But she had lived with walls of mud and a floor of cement at its best and so she insisted on the color white. She knew her sister was a little jealous—and that made it all the better!

It was not long before the big day—the day to move in.

The men from the city held a ceremony and gave her the keys to the house. The keys! She had never needed keys before. Then, they all went through room by room. The smaller grandchildren rolled on the soft rug. Her daughters went right into the bathroom and turned on the shower water. They flushed the toilet. They lingered, looking in the mirror and washing their hands. Angela looked forward to a winter in which no one would need to struggle outside in the cold to use the outhouse.

She wished Simon were here to see this. Maybe he would return again soon. She had given birth to eighteen children and only eight were still alive. She loved each of them for their uniqueness. No two were alike. Some were quick; some were slow. Some were easygoing; others had hot tempers. Now, maybe more would stay with her, arguing and fighting, but she would not be alone!

People had always asked her: "Why have so many children?" They didn't know—she loved each one of them. Maybe life was hard, but it was worth it.

She had an old bed to move into one room, a gas stove, and a treadle sewing machine that Simon had earned money to buy for her many years before. All the rest of her possessions fit into a medium-sized box. Things had come to her and flew away even faster—someone else wanted them more.

Her youngest son, Lazaro, was patient and had a way with plants. He promised to bring a rose bush and plant it for her. She liked flowers but had never had any that lasted long in the yard. Maybe they would have a lawn in front, like her sister had.

She loved to look out the front window. She could see herself sitting on the little front porch and waving to her friends that passed by. For so many, many years, this nice house had been an impossible dream and now it had come true.

35

Inez slumped in the desk in the back row of her History class, reading a library book. Usually she went unnoticed. She knew her new schedule. This was her last class of the day and then she would be free for soccer practice.

"Miss Palomar."

Startled out of the pages she looked up at her scowling teacher who now stood over her in the aisle.

"Would you answer, *pulleeeese*?" He said it with an ugly sneer.

"Would you please repeat the question?" She had no idea what he had been discussing.

"No. I'll call on someone who is listening." He cut her off.

She put away her book and studied his face. His blonde hair was receding and he combed it forward. She could see a small scar on his forehead. Inez had no idea why Mr. Jarvis was picking on her. She usually had no trouble getting along with her teachers. From the very first day when he called out her name he had stared at her in a strange way.

A lot of things puzzled her, here. It had not been long since they had moved here from Washington State. She listened to his presentation but he did not call on her again.

"Put everything away except your pen. We will have a quiz."

Good. She liked tests and when the paper was passed to her desk she was glad to see it was a multiple choice one.

She finished quickly but waited until others were done before handing in her paper. When the corrected tests were returned she saw she had missed two questions. This was better than most of her classmates.

She looked up to see Mr. Jarvis glaring at her. "Some people are not doing their own work. Miss Palomar, I am moving you to this seat in front."

Oh no. Did he really think she was cheating? She turned red as she moved to the front.

After that, she dreaded going to the class. Why was he so suspicious of her? She could think of nothing she might have done. She didn't really know anyone in the class to ask. In the front, she could no longer read a book or draw during class. He was always angry with her—only her.

The next time they took a quiz, she worked carefully, checked her work and turned it in—the first one. He corrected it, then, frowned at her. He got up from his desk and loomed over her.

How could he be suspicious? She was seated right in front of him. She knew he suspected her of cheating but couldn't understand how. He picked up her notebook and looked under it. There was nothing hidden. He made her feel very uncomfortable.

Now it was a game. She didn't say a word in class. During quizzes he would stomp around and hover over her while she whipped through the questions quickly, easily and handed them in first— long before the others. *How could she be cheating?* Mr. Jarvis grew angrier and angrier.

As she watched him she noticed something. If she made a sudden movement and he was near, he would flinch. So, every so often, she would jerk her hand or elbow. This was fun! She twitched and saw him back away. Then, she smiled at him. *But, why did he seem to fear her?*

On the last test of the semester she carefully checked her answers and turned in the paper. For this class she made sure to study. First again!

The next day he returned the papers. One of her answers was marked with a big red ex. She examined it, checked it again. It had to be right. She checked the textbook.

"Any questions?"

She raised her hand. "Mr. Jarvis, what is the answer to number eighteen?"

"President Madison." He growled.

"How is that possible? Doesn't the book say something different on page 245?"

"No! I'll show you." He opened the book with a triumphant look.

All around the room students raised their hands.

"Mr. Jarvis, Mr. Jarvis, I have something different, too."

"No!" He scanned the page, then, turned back to the class with a red face. "I guess the book says *Monroe*. If you have that answer bring your papers to me and I will give you credit."

Her mother attended open house at the school and visited with her teachers. When she returned that evening she told Inez, "I think Mr. Jarvis knew your Dad."

"Oh? I know he doesn't like me, but I don't know why. Did he say anything?"

"Not much. He was pretty gruff. He just asked me if my husband is named Simon. When I said *yes*, he was done talking."

Inez found her Dad in the garage, gluing a wooden chair. "Dad, do you know one of my teachers?"

He clamped the leg on the chair then turned. "What's his name?"

"Mr. Jarvis."

"Do you know his first name?"

"I've heard other teachers call him *Ron*."

Now he swung his head around to see her face. "Is he tall and blonde?"

"Yes, kind of blonde."

"I might know him from junior high." Her Dad looked concerned. "He doesn't give you a bad time, does he?"

"Sort of. But he's kind of afraid of me, too." She smiled.

"Well, I want you to know it's not your fault. If it's the same guy I remember we had a bit of a run in a long time ago. I'm afraid he probably hasn't forgotten what I did to him. If he bothers you any more, just let me know." He had a far-away-look in his eyes but said no more.

They walked together to the back of the house to watch another spectacular sunset to the west. There weren't many trees here but the skies were astonishing in their changing colors.

36

Celebration

(Much Later)

"Happy birthday to you!" They sang in tune and out of tune. Simon looked around the large table at his wife, his grown children and many grandchildren—big and small. One grandchild stood over six feet...the newest had not begun to crawl but sat giggling on his mother's lap. Despite his many failings God had blessed him immeasurably! He was richer than any millionaire.

He blew out the many candles in one breath. His heart was full to bursting with joy. As he fingered the presents he tried to guess each one. A crown! A plush crown. He put it on as well as the soft robe and felt like a king.

Hurdles and hardships had heightened his happiness. This was his birthday—not the day he was born but the anniversary of the day he quit drinking for good--forty years ago. He lived to see his children's children. And each of them was wonderful!

His own amazing children had far exceeded his expectations. Each one knew how to love and care for their children. His oldest, had gone from a paperboy to a Microsoft computer program designer. His second son, an engineer, a rocket scientist, traveled the world serving his country as a Commander in the Navy. His two beautiful, talented and treasured daughters were loving, thoughtful mothers of many children. They pampered him, too. And he couldn't have asked for better daughters-in-law or sons-in law!

There would always be some missing, among them—his son who had left this life too early....one whose time was a long story in itself. But, as he grew older, he knew that the day he would see them again grew closer.

He opened the last present and smiled—a water balloon slinger—and the day was warm and muggy. Storm clouds loomed to the west, but no rain fell as yet.

"Dad, balloons are ready outside."

"Who's on my team?" he asked as he stood to his feet, tossing his robe and crown to the side for the moment.

There was a mad dash to the backyard.

Made in the USA
Charleston, SC
25 May 2015